Chain,

King of the Wolves

To: Jamie
Best Wishes for
a long and
a happy life
Malinda Mitchell

Malinda Mitchell

PublishAmerica
Baltimore

First printing

ISBN: 1-4137-4048-0
PUBLISHED BY PUBLISHAMERICA, LLLP
www.publishamerica.com
Baltimore

Printed in the United States of America

DEDICATION

I would like to dedicate this book to my husband, Alton Mitchell, for believing in me; and to Publish America, for making my dream come true.

This short story is fictional in its entirety. Any similarity to names of people or events is coincidental.

Writing this and other stories are my way of getting the messsage across to people how harmful drugs are.

Introduction

Jack McCain found Chain while walking in the woods one cool fall day. The wind was blowing a cool, soft breeze and Jack was thinking what a shame it was that he was having to be searching for drugs in the woods when he could be at home, working in his yard. Jack had gotten a tip that someone was stashing cocaine in some old barrels in the woods, near an old shack. The location he was searching at was only ten miles from his home, so he knew the area pretty well.

During Jack's search, he heard a mournful little cry. He followed the sound to a bunch of bushes and there lay the most pathetic-looking little wolf pup you could ever imagine. He appeared to be about three months old and didn't look as though he had eaten in days. His hair was all matted and tangled, and he had cuts and scratches all over his little body.

Chapter One

Jack's drug tip was a false one, however little did he know that false lead would some day save his life. Chain would someday become his partner as an undercover drug investigator. Jack soon won Chain's love, respect and protection. However, Chain had a restlessness about him that no one would ever be able to tame.

Jack's housekeeper Mattie was afraid of Chain from day one. Just the idea of him being a wolf scared her. Even though Mattie was afraid of Chain, she grew to respect and admire the magnificent animal. Not only was Chain soon to earn the love and admiration of his master, but also the love and admiration of thousands of Americans.

After Jack found Chain and learned he had been pursuing a false lead, he gathered Chain up in his arms and took him home with him. Jack knew his housekeeper Mattie was afraid of big dogs unless she had known them since they were puppies. But since Chain was a puppy, she would be comfortable with him.

When Jack drove up in his driveway, Mattie came running out of the house with her arms waving in the air, screaming.

"Mr. Jack, Mr. Jack, your boss man down at the place where you work has been calling all morning. He wants you to call him as soon as possible. He says it's very important that you call him right away."

"Okay, Mattie, just keep your britches on. I'll go call him right now," Jack said.

Jack bent down and gently scooped Chain up into his arms and proceeded to hand him to Mattie. Mattie took one look at Chain and let out a yell, screaming.

"Oh no, Mr. Jack, you ain't about to get me to play nurse-maid to wild animals."

Jack took Chain and put him in a cardboard box on the back porch, and then hurriedly walked back into the house to phone his boss, Mr. Ralph Conners. As Jack picked up the phone to call Mr. Conners, he was wondering what wild goose chase he was going to send him on this time.

"It's about time you called me. I realize now that the tip you got earlier was a false lead. Someone is calling in false leads in order to keep us away from the real stash. Anyway, go to old Highway 46, to the old barn near the water tower, and look in that old tree trunk behind the barn. I just have a hunch about that place. I received a phone call saying that there is a lot of cars going in and out of there. It may not amount to a hill of beans but it never hurts to investigate. After all, that's our job," raved Mr. Conners after answering the phone on the first ring.

After Jack hung up the phone with Mr. Conners, he began to remember all the false leads he had been getting. Something was going on, but he just couldn't figure out what. Someone was trying to keep him occupied in order to protect their stash. Jack decided to keep his eyes and ears open and do a little investigating on his own, without Mr. Conners or anyone else knowing what he was up to.

In the meantime, there was a little pup that desperately needed his attention. Jack looked in the local telephone directory and found the number of a vet who wasn't far from his house and phoned him. The vet, Dr. Will Simon, agreed to see Chain right away once he heard what a bad shape the little fellow was in. Jack ran some warm bath water for Chain and found some baby shampoo that his sister had left a few months earlier when she and her two-year-old little boy had came for a week's visit. Allie's husband Jeff, an airline pilot, had to be gone longer than usual, so she figured that was as good a time as any to visit her big brother.

After running the water, Jack retrieved Chain from his box on the back porch and proceeded to put him into the warm bath water. Chain didn't like the water at first. However, once he learned that the water made him feel better he seemed to welcome the idea of a warm bath. Jack bathed the little pup, then dried him with a soft bath towel. Then he gently brushed and blow-dried his hair. He had to admit the grooming did wonders for the little pup's appearance.

Once the bath and grooming was completed, Jack took Chain to see Dr. Simon. Dr. Simon gave Chain all his first shots and worming and ointment for his cuts and scratches. He said the cuts weren't deep enough for sutures. After Dr. Simon assured Jack that Chain would be fine, Jack thanked him and made another appointment for Chain's second round of shots and worming, and then left for home. Once in the car Jack could already see the difference in Chain. He seemed friskier and happier. Jack looked at Chain with love in his eyes and said, "Chain, ole boy, Mattie Wiles has just got to love you now. You don't even look like the same pup. You are going to make me a fine partner someday. I'm going to teach you better than any animal has ever been taught anything."

Mattie was sweeping off the front porch when Jack drove up the driveway. She couldn't help but smile when she saw how clean and happy Chain looked.

"I'm sorry I missed Chain's bath, Mr. Jack," Mattie said sorrowfully. "I must have been outside raking up leaves in the backyard. I'm sorry I made such a scene when you brought the little pup home. It's just the idea of him being a wolf that frightens me. I'm sure I will overcome those fears in time. After all, he seems so sweet and gentle. By the way, Mr. Jack, your girlfriend called. She said she would call you again later today or in the morning. What's her name? Isn't it Wendy?"

"That's right," replied Jack. Jack smiled to himself as he remembered the first time he met Mattie. Her husband had just recently died. He had very little insurance and numerous medical bills. Mattie didn't have any skills. The only thing she knew how to do was cook and clean. Those two things she did very well. Mattie and her husband wasn't blessed with any children so Mattie tended to mother Jack. Jack met Mattie through a temp cleaning service. That was five years ago. Now, he just didn't know what he would do without her. He admited Mattie was a little nosey and sometimes bossy, however, that was just part of her charm.

When Mattie met Wendy, she just knew that she was the one for Jack. Wendy was working as a nurse in the emergency room at County General when Jack was rushed there by ambulance a couple of weeks after Mattie started working for him. Jack was shot in the shoulder during a drug bust. Mattie met Wendy when she was called to the emergency room after Jack was admitted.

Mattie took very good care of Jack after he was released from the hospital. She also played matchmaker for him and Wendy. She would call Wendy to come over to help her with first one thing or another. Finally, her matchmaking paid off. Once Jack was well enough to go back to work, he and Wendy started dating. Now, Mattie wondered why they didn't marry.

"Enough of this reminiscing," Jack thought as he picked up the phone to call Wendy. Jack really loved Wendy, however, he wasn't sure if she was completely over her ex- husband. Even though they had been divorced for a long time, Jack still had doubts. Wendy would let things slip out like, "Jim called today and said he and his new wife aren't getting along and he wants to come over and talk." Wendy divorced Jim Valley because of drugs, alcohol and other women.

"So why does Wendy feel the need to console Jim?" Jack wondered curiously. Jack also suspected Jim of some drug-related crimes that he had been investigating, and wondered how Wendy would react when the ---- hit the fan.

Jack walked slowly over to the phone and dialed Wendy's number. The phone rang only a couple of times when Wendy answered.

"Hello," said Wendy in a low, sultry voice.

"Hello," replied Jack nervously, because Wendy, after all this time, still took his breath away. Jack made a date with Wendy for the next day to go to a movie matinee. Sunday was his only day off that week. He felt fortunate that he was able to find a vet open on Saturday.

After he hung up the phone with Wendy, he sat down in his easy chair, then reached down and picked Chain up. The little fellow had been Jack's shadow ever since he bathed him. Jack just sat there, holding Chain and thinking about his life. He thought about his past. Jack was the eldest of two children. Allie and her husband Jeff were the only family he had. His and Allie's parents were killed ten years ago by a drunk driver. That's when Jack decided to become an undercover drug officer.

Jack had fond memories of his parents. His father was a postman and his mother was a homemaker. He and his sister Allie had always been close. All in all, he had been fairly happy, at least until that fatal car accident that claimed the lives of his parents. Jack was bound and determined to get rid of drugs in his home town.

CHAPTER TWO

It was Sunday morning, and Jack woke up early with his date with Wendy on his mind. He was also thinking about how to go about telling her his suspicions regarding her ex-husband Jim. He just had a gut feeling about him. After all, the man seldom worked yet he seemed to have all the comforts of a hard-working person.

While he thought, he got out of bed, walked into the bathroom, brushed his teeth and took a shower. Feeling all fresh and clean, he decided to sit down and think about what he would say to Wendy. He wanted to propose marriage to her, but he wanted to be sure of her feelings for him first. While he was thinking, he heard Mattie let out a yell that would curl hair. So he jumped up and ran in the direction that he heard the screams coming from, and found Mattie standing on the kitchen table and a dead mouse laying on the kitchen floor.

"Good grief, Mattie, a person would think you were being attacked," Jack said disgustedly.

"Mr. Jack, you know that I'm afraid of mice and rats and other varmints. I know they probably wouldn't hurt me, but they could sure cause me to hurt myself," Mattie replied.

"I swear Mattie, I don't know what in the world I'm going to do with you," Jack said.

"I try to overcome my fears, but it's hard to teach an old dog new tricks. By the way, Mr. Jack, will you be having lunch at home or will you be having lunch with your girlfriend?" Mattie asked.

"Mattie, it's amazing that you still can't remember Wendy's name. It's a very easy name to remember," Jack said.

"I know, Mr. Jack. That's another thing I need to work on. Fear of varmints, fear of dogs and remembering names. There wasn't much of a need for all these things when my husband was alive. I spend most of my time remembering what a good life I had before he passed away. I guess that keeps me from making any positive changes," Mattie said tearfully.

"I'm sorry, Mattie. I didn't mean to upset you. I didn't know that you still missed your husband that much. I'll try to be a little more understanding in the future," Jack said, while giving Mattie a big hug. "Anyway in answer to your question, I'll be having lunch and dinner in town so just fix yourself something to eat, and if you don't mind be sure and keep an eye on Chain for me. I'll be gone until sometime in the night," Jack said as he walked into the living room.

"I may just stay the night here, if you don't mind," Mattie said.

"You know you're always welcome, Mattie," Jack yelled out as he was walking out the front door.

Jack walked out to his car with keys in hand, feeling sorry that he had said anything to Mattie about her being so forgetful. After all, she was getting on in years. He smiled to himself as he thought about the love she felt for her husband. She still loved him after all this time. Jack hoped to someday have a wife who would love him that much, and hoped that it would be Wendy. On the way to Wendy's house, Jack noticed how beautiful the trees are during the fall of the year. He began to have fond memories of his parents. He remembered how they enjoyed taking long walks during the fall and spring months. Jack wondered why people wanted to mess up their lives, along with the lives of others, with drugs and alcohol. He knew he couldn't change the world, but he wanted to do whatever he could to make a difference. Little did Jack know, while he was doing all that thinking, that someday soon his life would change almost instantly. He would meet someone who would change his life forever. As Jack drove into Wendy's drive, he thought he caught a glimpse of someone running away from the back of her house. "Probably just my imagination," he thought. The drug searches, the suspicions of Wendy's husband and the doubts about some of his co-workers seemed to have his mind working overtime. He knew he needed to be more balanced with his work and personal life and he promised himself that he was going to do just that.

Jack parked his car behind Wendy's, turned off the engine, took his keys out of the ignition and slowly looked around Wendy's yard. He never noticed it before, but Wendy had a rather small front yard, and her backyard was only a hop, skip and a jump from a car wash. He never did like the fact that she lived in town. But she only lived a few minutes from her job.

As he knocked on Wendy's front door, he noticed her living room window was open. As he stepped back from the door, he thought he heard Wendy tell someone that she would see them tomorrow with the money. He felt like an eavesdropper, even though he wasn't trying to listen in on her conversation. Wendy told whoever she was talking to that she had to hang up and answer the door. He thought it odd that she didn't mention that she had a date, but decided not to let that bother him.

Wendy opened the door with a surprised look on her face. Even though she was beautifully dressed and her long auburn hair was flowing radiantly around her shoulders, she seemed as though she wasn't expecting company. Jack couldn't help but be stunned by her look of surprise.

"You do remember our date to go to the movie, don't you, Wendy?" Jack asked in a surprised tone of voice.

"I'm sorry, Jack, but I completely forgot. It has been one heck of a week at the hospital. Then when I get home I'm swamped with personal chores, numerous phone calls and it seems as though everyone I know wants a favor," replied Wendy, noticing Jack's shocked look.

"We can skip our date if you choose to do so," Jack retorted, even though he didn't intentionally mean to sound so sharp.

"No, no, that's perfectly okay, Jack. I'm dressed and ready to go. I'm just sorry I forgot our date. I apologize again for being such a do-do," Wendy said.

"Well let's get rolling," Jack said as he reached for Wendy's sweater that was hanging on a coat rack beside the door. As he proceeded to help Wendy put her sweater, on he couldn't help but admire her natural good looks. She didn't need make-up, even though she usually wore a little. She had beautiful brown eyes and cream-colored complexion. As he walked Wendy out to his car and opened the door for her, he remembered what Mattie said about if he and Wendy ever had children, that they would be beautiful.

"After all, with your being six feet tall and having a head full of jet black hair and beautiful green eyes and tan skin, and Wendy being so beautiful as she is, there isn't any chance of you having an ugly baby," he lovingly recalled Mattie saying. *That's one time Mattie remembered Wendy' name*, Jack thought. Once in the car, Jack noticed Wendy looked a little pale. He hadn't noticed it inside the house. *Should I mention her looking pale or should I keep it to myself? After all, she might get offended*, he

thought. So he decided to let the matter alone. After all, she seemed to feel alright.

Jack didn't like the movie and was ready to take Wendy home as soon as dinner was over. They skipped lunch since neither of them had been hungry. The day seemed to be a complete waste for Jack. He could sense something was going on with Wendy. She seemed edgy and he felt that she was keeping something from him. The thought occurred to him that her ex-husband might be bothering her and she might be ashamed to tell him.

Jack didn't like Jim. It wasn't because he was Wendy's ex-husband either. Well, maybe that played a small part in his negative feelings for the fellow. However, his gut feeling that Jim was hiding something played a much bigger role. Jack intended to keep a sharp eye on Jim and Jim's friends. He also intended to watch Wendy more closely too. She didn't look well to him. Her paleness could be from overworking or any number of things. Whatever the reason, Jack intended to be more thoughtful concerning her needs.

After dropping Wendy off at home, Jack decided to make a stop at the pet store to buy Chain a bed and a couple of pet toys. On the way to the store, he remembered what Ralph Conners had mentioned to him about Highway 46, the water tower and the old tree trunk behind the barn. He decided to stop at the pet store first and on the way home he would check out the tree trunk.

"I must have been hanging around Mattie too long. Her forgetfulness is rubbing off on me. I can't believe I forgot to check out that tree trunk on the way to Wendy's," Jack thought laughingly.

Jack stopped at the pet store and bought Chain a bed, a bone and a couple of little pet toys, paid the cashier and left. On his way to Highway 46 he couldn't help but wonder where Mr. Conners was getting all his information. He decided not to worry about that until he checked out this tree trunk.

Just as he thought, the tree trunk was another false lead – or maybe not. Propped against the tree trunk was a shovel with fresh dirt on it. Jack reached into his pants pocket and pulled out a glove and put it on. He always kept a couple of gloves in his pockets to prevent damaging evidence. He picked up the shovel, walked over to the car, opened the trunk and carefully laid the shovel in it. After closing the trunk he walked around the surrounding area to look for any fresh, loose dirt. He didn't see any so he decided to go home and call for help to search the area.

When Jack drove up into his driveway, he could hear Mattie yelling. He probably couldn't have heard her if his window had been up. Anyway, he turned off the engine, took out his key, opened the door, got out of the car and ran into the house as fast as his legs would carry him only to find Mattie kneeling on the kitchen floor beside a five-gallon washtub and thick rubber gloves that reached up to her elbows, giving Chain a bath.

"Mattie, what in the world are you doing?" Jack asked with a surprised look on his face.

"This little heathen puppy got out of the house without me seeing him and came back home covered in poop. Don't ask me where he got into it at because I don't have the foggiest notion. Anyways, that's why he's getting a bath and that's why the house stinks to high heavens and that's one of the reasons why I have on thick rubber gloves up to my elbows. Another reason for the gloves is that I don't want to get clawed to pieces by a stinky, nasty puppy," replied Mattie.

"I'm sorry Chain put you through this ordeal, Mattie, and I'm sorry I don't have time to help out, but I have to make an urgent phone call and go back to work," Jack said apologetically.

"I thought you were on a date," Mattie said.

"I was. However, I remembered something my boss wanted me to look into, so I dropped Wendy off and stopped off at the pet store and then I took care of business. That's something I should have done sooner. What's important now is that I make that phone call," Jack replied as he walked into the living room to use the phone.

As he dialed Mr. Conner's number, he couldn't help but wonder where the shovel came from and what or who had been buried, if either. The phone rang several times before Mr. Conners answered.

"Conners here," he answered gruffly.

"Hello, Mr. Conners. Jack McCain here. I checked out that tip you gave me earlier. I found a shovel with fresh dirt on it. I checked the surrounding area thoroughly and didn't see any fresh loose dirt, however I would like for you to send me some help to check the area a little further," Jack said with a sense of urgency in his voice.

"Go back to the spot where you found the shovel and wait. Help will be there when you arrive or shortly afterward. I'll be there shortly myself," Mr. Conners said as he hung up the phone.

"Mattie, I have to go back out. I don't know what time I will be back," Jack yelled as he walked out the door.

"Okay, be careful," Mattie yelled back.

When Jack arrived at the place he found the shovel, there were several other drug agents at the site. Mr. Conners arrived shortly after Jack got there and began giving orders for everyone to spread out and search the area. The team searched for three hours with flashlights and weapons in hand. They were just about to give up their search when Cliff Crowley, a fellow drug officer, spotted what appeared to be a freshly dug grave. The hole hadn't been long filled because the dirt was still loose. Cliff began yelling for everyone to come to the supposed gravesite. Once all the other officers arrived Mr. Conners gave orders for a couple of the officers to go get shovels and come back so everyone could begin excavating.

When the officers arrived with the shovels, the rest of the officers were handed one and they all began digging. About three feet into their digging they could see bits and pieces of a dark-colored bag of some kind. As they dug deeper, and as a couple of the officers who were shining light instead of digging shone more light into the hole, they could see that it was a large black garbage bag. More than likely, a body was inside. Once they retrieved the supposed body from the hole, they could see more clearly that it was two garbage bags covering the outline of what appeared to be a body of a person. One garbage bag had been put on from one end and the other from the other end, and a medium sized rope wrapped around the middle to hold them in place.

"Alright men, let's be prepared for anything. Get out your mask and gloves and put them on," ordered Mr. Conners. Once Mr. Conners put his mask and gloves on he ripped open the end of the bag that looked as though it concealed a head. When Jack saw the head of the corpse that was in the bag, he almost fainted. Mr. Conners gave orders for someone to escort Jack back to his car and stay with him until he regained his composure.

Jack walked slowly back to his car with Cliff by his side just in case he should faint. By the time he got back to his car he had regained his composure enough to tell Cliff that the body in the bag was none other than Wendy's ex-husband, Jim Valley.

"This is not going to be an easy case to solve,"Jack told Cliff.

"Why do you say that?" Cliff asked with a look of wonder on his face.

"You probably don't know this, Cliff ole boy, but Jim Valley was probably deeply involved in a lot of our local drug problems. That's one of the reasons Wendy divorced him. That, along with his womanizing and alcoholism,"replied Jack.

"Well, Jack, do you have any leads at all?" Cliff asked.

"I have a hunch or two, but nothing I can prove. I told you, this is going to be a hard one to solve," replied Jack

Once the body was removed from the crime scene, Mr. Conners gave orders to all the officers about what to do concerning the investigation. Jack's orders were to tell him everything he knew about the victim, Jim Valley. Jack told Mr. Conners everything he knew.

What Jack didn't know was that Mr. Conners knew more about Jim than he did. Jack didn't know that Mr. Conners had been fooling around with Jim's wife for quite some time. Jack was soon to learn a lot of things that would shake him up. When all the officers left the crime scene, Jack gathered up all his equipment and went home. On his way home, he decided to start taking Chain with him everywhere he went. After all, that would be the best way for him to learn. That would also give Mattie a break from Chain. Jack's thoughts were all jumbled up in his mind. One minute, Jack would be thinking how he wished Chain was older and the next minute, he was wondering who killed Jim Valley.

Mattie must have been looking out the window watching for Jack to come home because just as soon as he drove up into the yard she came running out onto the porch, all excited. Jack wondered what in the world she was doing up that late. After all, it was eleven o'clock at night. Whenever she stayed the night there, she was always in the bed by nine-thirty or ten o'clock. She must have gotten wind of the murder of Jim Valley. As soon as he opened the car door Mattie began talking excitedly from the porch loud enough for him and the neighbors two miles down the road to hear her.

"Mr. Jack, some man has been trying to get in touch with you. He says he has some news for you about how Jim Valley died. I just hung up with him. Says he'll call back in about an hour. He wouldn't leave his name or number. Mr. Jack, I don't like for you to be working with this case, it being your girlfriend's ex-husband and all," Mattie said nervously.

"Don't worry, Mattie. Everything will be fine," exclaimed Jack as he looked around for Chain. He was just about to call for him when he came running out of the kitchen with water dripping off his mouth. "Hey fellow," Jack said as he reached down and picked Chain up. Chain gave Jack a big lick on his hand as if to say, *I'm glad to see you.* The next day, Chain would be going to work with Jack.

Jack played with Chain while he waited for the mysterious caller to call again. He was just about to give up hopes of the man calling back when the phone rang.

"Hello," Jack said with a note of curiosity in his voice.

"Is this Jack McCain?" asked the mysterious caller.

"Yes it is," replied Jack.

"You don't know me and I don't know you, however I have heard a great deal about you. And one of the things that I've heard is that you are a person that can be trusted. I heard that you don't reveal your sources," the caller said nervously.

"You heard right," replied Jack.

"Then name a place that will be safe for us to meet and I will tell you what I know," said the caller, still sounding a little scared.

"Meet me at that little store across from the mall in the morning at eight o'clock," Jack said. "Will you recognize me when you see me?" Jack asked.

"Yes sir, even though I don't know you personally, I recognize you when I see you," the man replied.

"Do you want to tell me your name now or wait til morning?" Jack asked.

"Let's wait til morning," replied the man.

"Alright, see you then," Jack said as he hung up the phone. "Chain, ole boy, I'm glad you're going to work with me in the morning," Jack said as he reached down and patted the little pup on the head. "And I hope that man whatever his name is knows something that will help solve this case," Jack said, thinking out loud.

Later while stretched out comfortably in bed, Jack had all kinds of thoughts going through his head. Who is this mysterious caller? Who killed Jim Valley? One thing he did know and that was that he was going to take Chain to the place where Jim Valley's body was found and see if he could sniff out anything. He knew Chain was young, probably too young to be of much help; however he was going to start training him tomorrow. Jack dozed off while deep in thought and before he knew it morning had already arrived. He awoke before the alarm went off, jumped out of bed and went into the kitchen to see if Mattie had breakfast and coffee made. She did, and was on her way to knock on his door to see if he was awake.

"I was just on my way to see if you were awake, but now I see that you are. Your breakfast and coffee awaits you," Mattie said cheerfully.

"You're certainly in a good mood this beautiful fall morning," Jack said with a note of surprise in his voice.

"Don't sound so surprised, I'm happy most of the time," Mattie said while puttering around in the kitchen.

"You're right, you are a very happy soul, but what do we owe your happiness to this beautiful morning?" Jack asked.

"My niece Dani Bradie is coming for a visit. She's a secretary for an advertising company in Ohio. She's thirty years old, never been married and very ambitious. I haven't seen her for a number of years. I haven't got many relatives that are living and I was delighted to hear from Dani. We've managed to keep in touch by phone, but don't visit often," Mattie said.

"I'm happy that your niece is coming for a visit and I hope that I have the pleasure of meeting her," Jack said as he gulped down his last bit of coffee.

"You will get to do just that this afternoon, because she will be arriving by car around three or four o'clock. That is, if you're home before I go home. I won't be staying here while Dani is visiting. However, I will still come over to take care of your house and fix your dinner. And if you don't get to meet Dani today then you can meet her in the morning," replied Mattie as she removed the leftover breakfast from the table. Jack whistled for Chain as he got up from the table. Chain came bouncing happily to his master when he heard his whistle. Jack reached down and lovingly scooped Chain up into his arms, then reached for his jacket as he walked past the coat rack.

Even though it was a beautiful fall day he felt a little chill in the air when Mattie opened the kitchen door a little earlier to walk outside to feed the birds and squirrels. Mattie didn't like to see anyone or anything hungry. Jack took a deep breath and breathed in the cool fall air as he walked out onto the front porch, down the doorsteps and out to his car. As he was walking out to his car, he held out his left arm and looked at his watch and noticed it was a quarter before eight. He couldn't waste any time; he had to meet his mystery man in fifteen minutes. Sometime later he planned to take Chain out to old Highway 46 and let him sniff around a little.

Jack drove straight to the little store across from the mall. He usually bought his gas there and since he was a few minutes early he decided to fill up his tank. As he was replacing his gas cap he noticed a thin young man walking toward him. He was dressed in baggy clothes and wore an old brown cap. As the young man approached him he realized that he couldn't tell if he was a man, boy or girl. Whatever, the person was very young. "Maybe it wasn't the mystery man," he thought. The young looking person continued to walk in his direction and Jack noticed what seemed to be a look of caution on his/her face.

As the unknown person approached Jack he heard him/her ask in a girl's sounding voice, "Aren't you Jack McCain?"

"Yes I am," Jack replied.

"My dad was the one who called you. He couldn't come. He couldn't risk anyone recognizing him. I live in another state and don't anyone around these parts know me, and I don't want them to know me. That's why I'm dressed like a boy. My dad filled me in on everything. He also described you and your car to me," the girl said as she offered her hand for a friendly handshake.

"Do you mind telling me your name and your daddy's name?" Jack asked. "My name is Amanda Folds and my dad's name is Henry Folds. I live in Virginia with my mother. I'm old enough to live alone, however I choose not to. I came down to visit my dad last week and he has been filling me in on everything he knows about the drug problem in this town. When he heard about Jim Valley, he said he needed to tell you what he knows. He was in the woods that night and saw Jim get killed. He described the killer as being a man of medium height and a little overweight with a good-sized belly. Dad worked for the police force until his heart went bad. Now he just sits home and wishes he could work," Amanda said, rattling on.

"What police force did he work for?" Jack asked.

"He worked for the police force in West Virginia. He and my mom got a divorce when I was only five years old. He was always so wrapped up in his work that he never had any time for us. After they divorced, Mom and I moved to Virginia. Later, after Dad's heart attack, he decided to move here to this part of Georgia. He just sits at home most of the time and keeps up with the news. He also likes to go on nature walks. That's what he was doing when he saw Jim Valley get killed. Dad had really planned to come this morning but he backed out at the last minute. He knew wouldn't anyone expect me to be an informant. Anyway, I will be leaving town in the morning," Amanda said, still sounding nervous.

"You may have already told me but tell me again. If your dad doesn't know me, then how could he describe me to you?" Jack asked Amanda.

"He has seen you around and heard enough about you to know that you are a good person," replied Amanda.

"Thank you for the information and thank your dad for me, too. Also, tell him that I would like very much to meet him," Jack said as he gave Amanda's hand a farewell shake. After saying their good-byes Jack walked inside the store to pay for his gas. While inside the store, he looked out the window and saw Amanda drive away in a new silver Pontiac. It looked like another person was in the passenger's seat, but he couldn't see well enough to get a good look. Jack paid for the gas and walked back outside to his car. He opened his car door and found that Chain had urinated on his seat.

"I can see that I have another lesson to teach you, and that is my car is not the great outdoors," Jack said as he reached for some paper towels he had on his back seat. He had bought the towels for Mattie and had forgotten to give them to her. Now he was glad that he had forgotten. He was also glad that he had leather seats. When he finished cleaning his seat he threw the dirty paper towels in the garbage, got into his car and drove away.

After Jack left the store he decided to go to his office and look around. He already knew the person that fit the description Amanda gave him. But he just couldn't believe that person had anything to do with that crime. What Jack wanted to do now was to find out about Jim Valley's body.

When Jack walked into Mr. Conners office he found Cliff Crowley sitting at his desk. "What are you doing, sitting at the boss's desk?" Jack laughingly asked Cliff.

"I just walked in here and since the boss wasn't in I decided to see how it feels to sit at the chief's desk," replied Cliff.

"You'd better not let Mr. Conners catch you sitting at his desk, and you'd better not let him hear you calling him chief," Jack said in a stern voice.

"I didn't know he was that touchy. I had him pegged for an alright kind of fellow," Cliff said in a defensive tone of voice.

"He is an alright kind of fellow. He just has certain rules and I thought you knew them," Jack said as he motioned for Cliff to follow him outside. Once outside, Mr. Conners office Jack asked Cliff if he had heard any news concerning Jim Valley's murder. After learning that they had found cocaine and numerous other drugs in Jim's blood, and cocaine and marijuana in his pants' pockets, and that he had suffocated, Jack told Cliff to tell Mr. Conners that he would see him later on in the day. Jack wished Cliff a good day and walked outside, checked his seats for poop and urine, got into his car and headed for old Highway 46.

Jack looked down at Chain, rubbed his little furry gray head and said, "Chain ole boy, you and I are going to do some searching in the woods." Jack was thinking the entire time while driving about his conversation with Amanda Folds. He wondered why Henry Folds all of a sudden got cold feet about meeting with him. Jack was hoping that Mr. Folds would change his mind about talking with him and arrange another meeting. Still deep in thought, Jack saw the sign that read "Old Highway 46." He veered to the right and continued to drive while deep in thought.

Could Mr. Folds' description fit Ralph Conners? Jack knew that he somehow had to meet this Mr. Folds and get a little more information out of him. Chain jumped up on the passenger's door and put his little paws on the window and started to bark his little puppy bark as if to say, *We're here, let's get to work.* Because just about the time Chain started to bark Jack had reached his destination. Jack parked next to the old barn near the water tower, turned off the engine and got out of the car with Chain in his arms. When he was completely out of the car, he put Chain down on the grass. The very second Jack put Chain down on the grass, that little pup started sniffing and barking his little puppy bark and running around. Chain ran in the direction of the barn. Jack followed him into the barn. The big old red barn was old and the door had been missing for a long time. Chain ran in the direction of the hay loft barking while looking up toward the hay loft. Jack knew that Chain had either heard or smelled something, so he decided to climb the steps that led to the hay loft.

Just as he was about to reach the top of the steps he heard a faint cry. Jack hurried as fast as he could on his hands and knees, trying the entire time to be careful and not to hurt whatever or whomever that little cry was coming from. The closer he came to the faint little cry, the more it sounded like a baby. Jack only had to crawl a few more inches before he reached the source of the little cry. He found, wrapped in an old pink blanket, a newborn baby. The baby couldn't have been there very long because the umbilical cord was still attached to the infant. Jack unwrapped the infant enough to see that it was a little girl. She appeared to be healthy and maybe weighed seven or eight pounds. The little infant girl was chewing on her fist as if she was getting something out of it. Jack left the loft long enough to go to his car to call for an ambulance and Mr. Conners. As soon as he made his calls he returned to the hay loft and the infant girl. It seemed like an hour even though it was only a few minutes before the ambulance and Mr. Conners arrived.

When Jack heard the sound of the ambulance he climbed down the ladder to show the E.M.T.s where the infant girl was. He reached the barn door just as the ambulance arrived. He stood at the barn door and motioned for the E.M.T.s to come in his direction. The E.M.T.s got everything they needed to care for an infant child and hurried to the barn loft to tend to the infant. It only took a few minutes for the E.M.T.s to take care of the infant's immediate needs and get her in the ambulance and be on their way to the hospital with her.

Mr. Conners drove up just as the ambulance was leaving. He got out of the car and walked hurriedly over to where Jack was standing. "What in the world is going on?" Mr. Conners demanded to know at once. Jack explained everything that happened up until the time of Mr. Conner's arrival.

"You mean to tell me that your little puppy saved that little baby's life?" Mr. Conners asked in a shocked tone of voice.

"That's exactly what I'm telling you. If I hadn't brought Chain out here today, that little girl would be dead tomorrow,"replied Jack in a proud voice. Jack wasn't only proud of Chain, but he was also proud and happy that the little baby was alive and was going to have a chance at life.

Chain had become a star overnight. The head lines read, "Drug Enforcement Agent's Little Puppy Saves Newborn Infant's Life." Jack couldn't have been prouder of anything or anybody than he was of Chain. He knew now for certain that Chain had sharp ears and a keen sense of smell. He just hoped that his name didn't get revealed and his chances of working as an undercover investigator blown. Jack knew that he and the rest of the law enforcement had their work cut out for them. Somehow, Jim Valley's murder, the drug smuggling and the newborn infant was connected – or so he thought. He didn't know how just yet, but he was sure as heck going to find out.

CHAPTER THREE

A couple of months passed, and Chain grew like a weed. The hospital did blood work on the Jane Doe infant. The infant had probably been born at home. Jim Valley's blood was checked and he was ruled out as the father. Jack was still watching Mr. Conners closely and carefully followed him to Candy Valley's house. Jack just assumed that Mr. Conners was getting information concerning her late husband, Jim Valley, until he overheard a little office gossip about Mr. Conners and Candy Valley's affair while her husband Jim was alive. Jack later asked Cliff Crowley if he knew anything about Mr. Conners having an affair with Candy Valley.

"Yes, man. Do you mean to tell me that you didn't know Mr. Conners was having an affair with Jim Valley's old lady?" Cliff asked in a shocked voice.

"I don't know how I missed the gossip all this time, but I sure didn't know anything about that affair until recently when I overheard some office gossip," replied Jack.

"I don't know how you missed it either, because that was going on for a while before Jim got knocked off," Cliff said in a smug tone of voice.

"Well, thanks a lot for the info," Jack said as he turned and walked away. "Whatever got into Cliff?" Jack wondered. He hadn't ever thought of Cliff as a smug person.

As Jack walked into his office, he was mentally trying to put all the pieces about what he had just learned together. Was it possible that Mr. Conners could somehow be involved in all this mess? And if he was, then how, and how much? Jack knew that he needed to talk with Henry Folds, and soon. He opened his desk drawer and got out the local telephone directory and began looking in the F section for Henry Folds. He found one Henry Folds living at 333 Cleveland Avenue. Jack decided not to call him. Instead, he would make a surprise visit.

At the end of the day Jack checked his office to see if Chain had made any messes on the floor, got his leash off the desk and hooked it to Chain's collar and made tracks for the parking lot. He was ready to pay Mr. Henry Folds a visit. That address wasn't far from his office, so he could just make a loop and see if anyone was at home. When Jack got out to the parking lot he noticed the same car that Amanda Folds was driving the day he met her, leaving from across the street. That had been the only new silver Pontiac he had seen in town, so she must still be in town or she was making a return visit. Jack walked slowly over to his car while watching the silver Pontiac turn in the opposite direction that he was about to go. "Well, I haven't got time to follow her. I have to take care of the business at hand, then go home and get ready for my date with Wendy. Then tomorrow I have to meet Mattie's niece. I didn't get to meet her the last time she was here for a visit and Mattie's feelings was very hurt. She said that it was perfectly alright, but I knew better," Jack said, thinking out loud. "I'm sure that you don't want to hear all my plans, do you, Chain ole boy," Jack said as he rubbed Chain's back lovingly.

While Jack was opening his car door he noticed a note on his windshield. He picked it up after putting on a glove and the note read, "You will never catch me." Jack had gotten all kinds of little notes during his years as a law enforcement officer. He had gotten even more since he had been working in the drugs department. He got an unused plastic bag out of his dash and put the note in it. This note would be used as evidence along with all the other evidence that was piling up. Next, he told Chain to get in the car and then he got in the car and drove in the direction of 333 Cleveland Avenue.

When he arrived at 333 Cleveland Avenue, he didn't see the silver Pontiac. That didn't really surprise him, though. Jack parked the car near the curb on the side of the road, got out of the car while telling Chain to stay in the car. Chain was very obedient, even though Jack could detect a restlessness about him. Chain sat still while Jack walked up the steps that led to Henry Folds' house. Jack was thinking how Mr. Folds must have made a very good living when he was able to work, because this was a very nice neighborhood and the houses in that section of town were very nice. When he reached to ring the doorbell the front door opened and a man that very much resembled Mr. Conners was standing there, looking shocked. He apparently was about to leave and didn't notice or hear Jack's car when he drove up in front of the house.

Jack introduced himself and made a polite gesture to shake the gentleman's hand. "Good afternoon sir, I'm looking for Mr. Henry Folds. Would you, by any chance, be him?" Jack asked.

"Why are you looking for Mr. Folds?" the gentleman asked while shaking Jack's hand.

"I need to ask him a few questions about a case I'm working on. I spoke with someone a while back that claimed to be the daughter of this Henry Folds. If you are in fact this person, then I can assure you that any information you give me will be kept confidential," Jack said reassuringly.

"Yes, I'm the person you're looking for. I was just about to leave and wouldn't have opened the door had I known you were standing there," Mr. Folds said nervously. Jack could see the man's hands were shaking and knew that Mr. Folds was probably not going to reveal all his information at once. He was more than likely going to have to make a few return visits to get Mr. Folds to tell everything he knows. "My daughter told you exactly what I would have told you," Mr. Folds said in a shaky voice.

"Mr. Folds, if you don't feel up to talking I can come back another day. Your daughter told me that you have a heart condition," Jack said sympathetically.

"I'm only going to say one thing and then I must rest. The person that you are looking for works with you. He is very clever and respected in the community. You will have to take my word for this," Mr. Folds said as he held the door open for Jack to leave.

Jack thanked Mr. Folds for his time and turned and walked out the door. As he was walking out to his car he was thinking how his life had changed since he found Chain. Even though he was supposed to be an undercover drug investigator, he found himself doing all kinds of investigating. While still deep in thought Jack opened his car door and got in without thinking to check his seat for poop and urine. He had also forgot to take Chain for his nature walk earlier. Jack no sooner sat down than he felt something squashy between his bottom and the seat. He knew instantly what had happened. "Doggone it, Chain, couldn't you have held on just a little while longer? Now I have to sit in this mess until I get home. I'm afraid to move, because if I move the odor will be worse than it is now. Doggone it," Jack said, repeating himself.

Jack tried to get his thoughts back to how his life had changed since he had found Chain. At least thinking about that would help get his mind off the mess he was sitting in. Since Chain had found the little Jane Doe infant, the news articles had been in numerous newspapers. His phone rang so much he got caller ID installed. That way he only had to answer the important calls. It didn't take long for his undercover investigating to be uncovered. He hoped they would find the little baby's mother soon. Most people want to know a little something about an infant's parents before adopting it.

Still deep in thought, Jack noticed he was almost home. "Thank God for small favors. Only this seemed to be a big favor. Now I can get this stinking mess off me and take a much-needed shower. Mattie thinks she loves me like a son. Let's see how much she loves me when she sees and gets a whiff of this mess," Jack said, thinking out loud. He was still mumbling under his breath as he drove up into his driveway. He put the car in park, took the keys out of the ignition, opened the car door and slowly got out of the car. Getting out of the car slowly didn't help keep the odor down, though. As soon as he stepped out of the car he ran in the direction of the water hose. He was desperately hoping to get the poop off of himself before Mattie saw him. No such luck. Mattie must have been just around the corner of the house because just before he reached down to pick up the spray nozzle that was attached to the hose Mattie made an appearance.

"What in the world is that all over the seat of your pants? Never mind, you don't have to answer that," Mattie said while laughing so hard that Jack thought she would burst a gut.

"This is not funny," Jack said with a look of embarrassment on his face.

"I know it shouldn't be, but you aren't seeing it from this side of the scenery," Mattie said while trying not to laugh.

Jack hosed himself off the best he could and then walked over to his car and opened the back door thinking how good it was that he still had that roll of paper towels laying on the back seat. While he was rolling off a handful of towels he couldn't help but notice that Chain hadn't moved from the spot he was in since they got home.

"What are you doing, Chain? I guess you're waiting for me to clean up this awful mess before you get out of the car. Are you afraid you will get some of your poop on yourself? Or are you hoping that I will get some more on myself?" Jack asked Chain in a disgusted tone of voice. "Well, I haven't got time to figure out your personality flaws. I have to get ready for my date with Wendy and I hope to solve some of our problems tonight. Furthermore I don't know why I'm standing here having a conversation with you," Jack said as he cleaned up the last of the poop.

Meanwhile, inside the house, Mattie was gathering up the disinfectant and some old rags to take outside to help with the poop cleaning-up chore. She also grabbed Jack some old clean shorts to put on so he wouldn't have to wear dripping wet clothes inside the house.

As soon as Mattie walked back outside and took one look at Jack, she began laughing again. She was still laughing when she handed him the clean pair of shorts. "Here Jack, take these shorts and go back to your shop and put them on. Take your wet clothes off first though," she said, still laughing.

"I'm not a complete fool; I do have enough sense to remove wet clothes before putting on dry ones," Jack said as he reached to take the shorts from Mattie's outstretched hand.

"I know you do, honey," Mattie said as she began doing the touch-up cleaning on Jack's car seat.

"You could have fooled me," Jack said, as he turned and walked away.

Mattie was still laughing to herself when she noticed that Chain was still sitting on the front passengers seat. Chain still made Mattie a little nervous, and more than likely he always would. Seeing Chain sitting on the front seat of Jack's car calmed Mattie's laughter.

"You can get out of the car now, Chain," Mattie said nervously as she stepped aside so he could come bounding out.

Chain got out of the car with one big leap once the seat was cleaned and headed toward the house. He stood at the back door and waited for Jack or Mattie to open the door so he could go inside and eat. It didn't take Jack long to get into some dry clothes, so Chain didn't have to wait at the door but a few seconds. Jack opened the back door and Chain made a dash for his food bowl only to find it empty. He made one quick bark to alert Jack to his need for food.

"You know what amazes me, Chain?" Jack asked as he filled Chain's bowl with food. "Well of course you don't – and then again maybe you do. You crap in my seat and then you move over to the clean side of the car and sit there until all of your poop is cleaned up and now you want me to give you something to eat so you can poop some more. You are one rotten dog, or should I say, wolf," Jack added.

Mattie opened the back door and stepped inside the kitchen during Jack's one-sided conversation with Chain. "Has Chain started answering you yet?" Mattie asked with a little chuckle.

"Yes. He told me to tell you to be nice to me and to quit being afraid of him," Jack replied with a little note of humor to his voice.

"I'll try," Mattie said laughingly.

"This has been a blast, but all good things must come to an end. You had better hurry up and get ready for your date with Wendy. See, I didn't forget her name. And don't you forget that you have to meet Dani in the morning. You can come over around nine and eat breakfast and meet Dani at the same time," Mattie added.

"Call me around eight or a quarter before eight just to make sure that I'm out of bed and haven't forgotten," replied Jack.

"Will do," Mattie said lovingly.

With the reminders out of the way, Jack headed for the bedroom to get clean clothes and underwear to take with him to the bathroom so he could take a shower. He still felt stinky and was anxious to take a shower so he could feel clean again.

In the meantime Mattie was finishing her final chores for the day while thinking pleasant thoughts about her relationship with Jack. She didn't think she could love him any more if he were her own son. Of course, she would never know for sure since she and her husband had been childless. After she finished wiping the kitchen counter, she grabbed her purse and sweater and yelled out to Jack that she was going home and that she would call him in the morning. She could barely hear his reply of a quick, "Okay."

"See you later, Chain," Mattie said as she walked hurriedly out the back door. She was in a hurry to get home and attend to her own chores.

No sooner than Mattie had walked out the door than the phone rang. Jack couldn't hear the phone ringing with the shower running and he had no way of knowing that the call was of the utmost importance. Chain tried to answer the phone by knocking it off the hook with his left front paw, while barking the entire time as if to say, *I'm trying to help.*

Jack heard Chain barking as he turned off the shower. He hurriedly got out of the shower while grabbing a towel to wrap around himself, just in case Mattie hadn't left to go home yet. What he found when he walked into the livingroom was Chain laying sprawled out on the floor holding the phone between his two front paws.

"I need you for a partner, not a secretary. Give me that phone," Jack told Chain jokingly as he took the phone away from him and put in back on the hook. He headed back in the direction of the bathroom without thinking to check the caller ID.

Once back in the bathroom, Jack shaved and put on fresh clean clothes and after shave lotion. Then he picked up his dirty clothes and wiped up the puddles of water on the bathroom floor. After he cleaned up his mess, he took his dirty clothes to the utility room. He didn't want Mattie to have to clean up his mess when she came back to work. Even though she was his employee, he didn't want to take advantage of her.

Jack was just about to check Chain's water bowl when he heard a knock on the door. He went ahead and quickly filled the water bowl, then walked in a fast pace to the front door wondering the entire time who could possibly be knocking at his door, while at the same time wondering why they didn't ring the doorbell. He peeked out the window on the front door before opening the door to see who the visitor was. He was surprised to see Ralph Conners standing on his front porch with a sad look on his face.

"What's wrong, Mr. Conners?" Jack asked as he opened the door.

"Do you mind if I come in?" Mr. Conners asked in reply.

"Of course not," Jack quickly answered.

"Jack I tried to call you a little while ago to see if you were at home and Chain answered the phone. I haven't been able to get him to talk to me yet," Mr. Conners said trying to add a little humor to the conversation, while trying to decide how to tell him what he so much hated to tell him.

"Sit down Jack, I have to tell you something and I don't know how," Mr. Conners added.

"Well for heaven's sake, man, just tell me," Jack said in a desperate tone of voice.

"Sit down first," Mr. Conners quickly replied.

"Okay, if it will speed things up. I have a date with Wendy and I'm in a hurry," Jack said.

"Jack, I hate to tell you this, but Wendy died about an hour ago. She was coming out of the bathroom at work and just fell over. The doctors say she was probably dead before she hit the floor. They found a used hypodermic syringe in her jacket pocket along with a bottle of morphine. A blood test will have to be performed and possibly an autopsy. I don't have all the details yet," Mr. Conners said as he walked over to the sofa where Jack was sitting and reassuringly put his hand on Jack's shoulder. "Is there anything I can do?" Mr. Conners asked as he removed his hand from Jack's shoulder.

"No, but thanks for asking. Right now I would just like to be alone. Thanks for taking the time to come and tell me the bad news in person," replied Jack.

"If there is anything at all the guys in the department or I can do, please feel free to ask," Mr. Conners said sorrowfully. Jack stood up and in a dazed state walked Mr. Conners to the door, and thanked him again for his thoughtfulness.

As soon as Mr. Conners left, Jack gave way to tears. He just sat down on the floor beside Chain and cried until he couldn't cry anymore. Chain gave a mournful little whine as if to say, *I'm sorry you feel sad.* Jack reached over and rubbed the fur on Chain's back and said, "I know you would take all the pain away if you could."

After Jack cried all he could cry, he stood up and went to the bathroom and washed his face. "Why in the world is all this bad stuff happening at once," Jack said aloud to himself. When he finished washing and drying his face and hands, he picked up the phone to call Mattie but then decided that she didn't need to hear news like this over the phone. He decided to go by her place on the way to the hospital. He wasn't sure where Wendy's body would be, but he just assumed it would still be at the hospital.

On the way to the hospital Jack began to remember how pale Wendy had looked for the past few months and she had been losing weight. He was wondering if she could have really been sick and just didn't tell anyone. Wendy didn't like to talk very much about her family even though she saw her sister Marlene occasionally. Even though he and Wendy had dated for over five years he had never met any of her family. Jack figured a next-of-kin would be on her job application. He hoped the hospital would take care of all that because he didn't know if he was emotionally up to the task. Jack was so deep in thought that he almost forgot to go by Mattie's house to tell her about Wendy. Mattie liked Wendy and he knew that she would be all broken up, just as he was.

As Jack slowly approached Mattie's house he could feel the tears begin to fill his eyes again. He wondered how long he would cry and why did Wendy have to die so young. She was only twenty-eight years old, a registered nurse with a promising future. *What in the world was going on,* he wondered.

Mattie was raking leaves when Jack arrived at her house. Jack got out of his car and slowly walked over to where Mattie was raking leaves. "Mattie, let's go sit on the porch swing for a few minutes. I have to tell you something," Jack said as he reached out and took hold of her arm to lead her to the porch. They walked slowly together, Mattie knowing the entire time that she was about to hear something that she would rather not hear, even though she knew that she must hear it. They sat together side by side on the swing while Mattie waited patiently to hear the bad news. Mattie broke down and cried when she heard the news. Jack stayed with her until he was sure that she was going to be alright. He also reassured her that he would be there the next morning to meet her niece.

"You don't have to visit me in the morning, after all that has happened today," Mattie said, all choked up.

"Wendy wouldn't want you or me to quit living. She would want us to go on with our lives as usual," Jack said reassuringly.

"You're right of course. She was that kind of a person," Mattie said lovingly.

"Anyway Mattie, they probably won't have her body ready for burial until tomorrow afternoon," Jack said.

"Alright Jack, you know best," Mattie said trustingly. Jack gave Mattie a big hug and a kiss on the cheek and then left for the hospital.

When Jack arrived at the hospital he decided to park in the emergency room parking lot. It was a rather large parking lot and there wasn't very many cars parked in it, so he figured it would be alright to park there for a little while. After he parked, he got out of the car and locked the doors and hurriedly walked toward the emergency room door.

As Jack approached the emergency room he could see Mr. Conners standing at the door as if he was waiting for him or someone else. Jack had barely gotten inside the door before Mr. Conners asked him how he was feeling and told him that Wendy didn't have any next-of-kin listed on her job application. She and Jim Valley were married when she first went to work there, but later had gotten a divorce. Apparently they weren't married very long.

Mr. Conners and Jack were still talking when the pathologist and coroner interrupted their conversation. Wendy had terminal cancer and was obviously injecting herself with morphine for pain. She had obviously been seeing a doctor in another city. The morphine she was taking was prescribed for her. She must have wanted to keep working to help keep her mind off her problems because she could have gotten disability and other assistance.

After the pathologist and coroner filled them in on everything, Jack and Mr. Conners walked outside to Jack's car. Jack told Mr. Conners that he was going over to Wendy's place and see if he could find any answers as to why she kept all this to herself. Mr. Conners asked if he wanted some company but Jack said that he would rather be alone. The pathologist and coroner didn't know if Wendy accidentally overdosed or if she overdosed on purpose. Someone else was investigating Wendy's case and Jack welcomed the help.

During Jack's drive to Wendy's, Mr. Conners popped into Jack's mind. It was hard for Jack to believe that he could do anything crooked. So what if he was and had been for some time been fooling around with Candy Valley; that didn't make him a drug pusher or a murderer. Jack's thoughts of Mr. Conners were interrupted by seeing Wendy's house. It seemed odd, not seeing her car parked in the driveway.

"Anyway, I'll just park where I always do and go inside and try to see if I can find something to help me make some kind of sense out of all this," Jack said while thinking out loud.

Once inside the house, he looked around and couldn't find anything out of the ordinary, so he walked outside and looked around and still didn't see anything so he decided to lock her door and go on home. Wendy had given him a key to her house sometime earlier, but he had never used it until now. Jack locked the doors and walked back to his car. He opened the door to his car and almost started to check for poop when he remembered that he didn't bring Chain along with him this time.

On the ride back to his house Jack wondered why Wendy hadn't told him that she was sick and even more so why he didn't inquire more as to how she was feeling. After all, he could tell she was losing weight and that she was looking pale. But terminal cancer? One other thing that was bugging Jack was why was Wendy still keeping in touch with her ex-husband before he was killed. Was he supplying her with some kind of illegal pain killers, or was she still trying to get him to straighten up his life? He decided to believe that she was just trying to get him to live a good life and let it go at that.

"Well, home again," Jack said as he drove up into his driveway. He parked his car, turned off the engine, got out and locked his car door. All these things he did out of force of habit. But how was he going to get out of the habit of loving Wendy? She may have been a better person than anyone realized. Everyone knew that she was a good nurse and dedicated to her profession. Jack gave way to tears again before he even unlocked his front door. He opened the door to find Chain standing near the telephone table, looking sorrowful. Jack put his keys back in his pants pocket and walked over to Chain and knelt down beside him and gave him a big tearful hug.

"Why didn't you come running to meet me, Chain ole boy? Do you feel sad because your best buddy is sad?" Jack asked as he hugged Chain even tighter. "Well, it's time to start trying to pull myself together," Jack said as he stood up while wiping the tears from his eyes and face with his shirt tail.

Just as Jack turned to walk into the kitchen to find something to eat and to fill Chain's food bowl he realized that he hadn't checked the mail box. He decided to fill Chain's food and water bowl, check the mail and then he would try and eat something. After he took care of Chain he stepped outside to check the mail. He reached inside the mail box and pulled out a handful of mail. The outside light was too dim for him to read so he walked back inside and laid the mail on the kitchen table while looking at the clock on the kitchen stove.

"Eleven-thirty!" Jack exclaimed. "I'll go through this mail in the morning. Right now I have to get some sleep. I'll eat in the morning too," Jack said, continuing to talk to himself. Jack didn't know that in that handful of mail was a letter that would warm his heart in a way that it had never been warmed before.

While still wiping an occasional tear Jack took the necessary steps to get ready for bed. Chain had been fed and now all he had to do was try and get some sleep.

The next morning Jack awoke with new-found energy. He must have really been exhausted because he slept like a baby. For a little while he forgot all the pain he had felt in his heart, soul and mind and actually slept. He made his way into the kitchen and let Chain out to take care of his morning business. Chain was beginning to get more and more restless and that worried Jack. He had hoped that being loved and taken care of would take the wild out of him, but it hadn't. The older Chain, got the more he wanted to run toward the woods. Sometimes at night Jack would awaken to hear Chain howling. If it wasn't such a sad howl, it wouldn't have bothered him so much. Jack stood and watched Chain as he tried to find the perfect spot to relieve himself of yesterday's food. Once he had taken care of business, Jack tried to persuade him to come back inside the house.

"Here Chain," Jack called while walking toward the house. Chain took one last glance at the woody area behind Jack's house, then turned his attention to Jack and obediently followed him inside the house. Jack closed the kitchen door once he was sure Chain's tail was out of the way and wouldn't get caught in it, then walked over to the table and pulled out a chair and sat down.

"Might as well go through the mail and see what kind of junk I got," Jack said to himself as he sorted through the different-sized envelopes. Among the junk mail and bills was a small-sized pink envelope with no return address. He decided to lay it aside until he finished going through his bills and putting them in their proper place. He had a little wooden box with dividers in it that he kept his bills in. One was for the first of the month and so on. When he finished putting his bills in their proper place, he put the junk mail in the garbage can and sat down at the table and picked up the little pink envelope. The envelope was small but thick. Jack decided to quit wondering who the letter was from and open it up and find out.

He opened the envelope and saw that the letter was written on pink stationary paper. The suspense was killing him, so he decided to look on the last page to see who it was from. His hands began to shake when he saw it was from Wendy. He could feel a lump begin to form in the pit of his stomach as he returned to the first page of the letter. It read:

My Dearest Jack;

It's with all the love that I have in my heart that I write you this letter. There was no way that I could look into your beautiful green eyes and tell you something that I know would break your heart. So writing you a letter is easier for me.

I've been battling cancer for a long time. I have incurable leukemia and I'm also having a lot of muscle and bone pain. I didn't tell you about my problems because I wanted the time we spent together to be filled with joy and laughter.

Winter will be over soon and spring is right around the corner. I know how much you like spring. Plant some beautiful tulips and yellow roses and remember me when they bloom. Please meet someone else that will appreciate and love you as much as I do.

Jack darling, I know you had your doubts about me and my feelings for Jim, but let me put your mind at ease. I only wanted him to grow up and be a responsible person. I also knew that if he continued drinking and doing drugs that he would someday have to pay the price. Of course it happened a lot sooner than I expected. Don't try to find my family because I don't have any that I want in my life. As far as I'm concerned you and Mattie are the only family that I have.

Please do as I ask. Be happy, love, laugh and enjoy your life because you're not promised tomorrow. By the time you read this letter I will be pain-free. I didn't want to die at home because I knew you would be the one to find me. The hospital seemed to be the best place. I felt so sick all the time that I knew my working days were almost over and I didn't want to be a burden on anyone, so I chose to end my pain the only way I saw fit. I hope you will forgive me for not confiding in you, but as I said I wanted our time together to be happy times.

Kiss Mattie good-bye for me and give Chain a hug and a kiss for me. You have a wonderful friend in that fine animal. Maybe one day he will quit being so restless.

I really don't know what I would have done without you. You have been the greatest friend I've ever had. If things had been different I know that someday we would have been married. But I want you to find a nice woman and fall in love again and get married. You're a good man and deserve to be loved, so when you finish reading this letter put it away and get on with your life. If ever you have any doubts about your worthiness to be loved, read this letter again, because you do deserve to be loved. When you fall in love again then it will be time to throw this letter away. You will fall in love again and be happy.

Now you know all you need to know about me. Plant flowers in the spring and watch them grow. Love, laugh and enjoy life and remember that you were loved by me. Don't forget how to love. Make yourself a promise right now that you won't forget how to love.

Remember me with love,

Wendy

Jack finished reading Wendy's letter with tear-filled eyes and a heart filled with more warmth and love than he had ever known. He loved her when she was alive, but he loved her even more now. He grew to know and love her more after her death than he did the entire time they dated. He would never have dreamed anyone could be so caring.

He got up from the table with letter in hand and walked wearily toward his bedroom. Where would he put Wendy's letter, he wondered. Under his mattress seemed like a safe place, so that was where he put it. Jack made up his mind right then and there to never tell anyone that Wendy took her own life. That was a secret that he would carry with him to his grave. Some things were better left alone, and that was one of those things.

After carefully placing Wendy's letter under his mattress, Jack remembered that he had to meet Mattie's niece. Even though he wasn't up to it, he took a shower and put on fresh clean clothes. Before he left for Mattie's, Jack made sure that Chain had plenty of food and water. He also took him outside for another nature walk. "I promise not to stay gone long. When I get home I will let you play and run until it gets dark," Jack promised Chain as he escorted him back inside the house. Jack closed and locked the door behind him as he left for Mattie's place.

Mattie had breakfast almost finished when Jack got there. Jack could smell the bacon cooking as he approached her backyard. "Mattie must have her kitchen window up," Jack thought out loud ás he continued to walk in the direction of her kitchen door. Jack loved to smell bacon cooking, and Mattie could cook some good bacon. Her bacon was always crisp and brown and never greasy.

Mattie was standing at the kitchen sink rinsing her hands and looking out the window when she caught sight of Jack walking toward the kitchen door.

"Come in, sweetheart," she called out to him just as he reached out to knock on the door.

"That bacon sure smells good cooking," Jack said, sounding hungry.

"I have biscuits, eggs and bacon all ready to be eaten. Coffee is ready to be poured and Dani should be walking in here at any second. You will like her, she's a nice girl," Mattie said, hoping to make Jack feel a little better. Mattie was just about to say something else when Dani walked softly into the kitchen. Mattie with dish towel still in hand introduced Jack to Dani and told them both to sit down and eat.

During breakfast, Jack couldn't help but notice that Dani was a very beautiful young woman. She didn't look anything like he had pictured her in his mind. When Mattie said that she was a very ambitious secretary, he automatically formed a mental picture of her as being a plain, somewhat mousey young woman. He didn't know why, because he normally didn't form opinions of people before meeting and getting to know them.

Dani had short blonde hair, beautiful blue eyes and clear ivory complexion. She also had beautiful full lips which he thought added to her beauty. At another time he might have been very much attracted to her, but right now he couldn't imagine being attracted to another woman in a romantic sense. Jack finished his breakfast, thanked Mattie for asking him over and told Dani that it was a pleasure meeting her and left for home. Mattie told him that she understood as she walked him to the door. They said their good-byes and he left. He had planned to go to the hospital to see Wendy, but that would be a waste of time since her body would be moved to the funeral home before noon.

As Jack walked to his car, he silently hoped that he wasn't being rude by leaving so soon. He had never been the sort of person to go to someone's house and just eat and leave. If he had stayed any longer, he would have been crying in his food. Wendy's body was being moved to the funeral home sometime this morning. They decided not to do an autopsy since the extensive blood work told them everything they needed to know. Everyone assumed that Wendy just accidentally overdosed because she was in so much pain. Since Wendy didn't put any next-of-kin on her job application, Jack was having to take care of everything. All of this was going through Jack's mind as he walked out to his car. Jack still couldn't figure out how to get in touch with Wendy's sister Marlene.

The drive home seemed to take a little longer than usual. As he was parking his car in the driveway he could see Chain peeking out the living room window. Jack wondered how long he had been looking out it. Chain looked so cute. He looked like a little child waiting for his/her daddy to come home from work.

Chain came bounding toward Jack as he opened the front door to come inside. Jack knelt beside Chain as usual and gave him a big warm hug. "Come on, boy. Let's go into the kitchen and check your food and water bowl," Jack said while patting Chain on the head. Chain gave a playful little growl as he obediently followed Jack into the kitchen.

After Jack attended to Chain's needs, he walked into his bedroom and took out the letter Wendy had written to him out from under his mattress and just held it without reading it. Tears began to fill his eyes again as he wondered how he could have her beautiful body cremated; but that was what she wanted. As Jack remembered some of his and Wendy's conversations, he knew that she was slowly preparing him a little at a time for her death. She would make little comments every now and then about what she wanted when she died. They were few and far between, but Wendy knew that he would remember when the time came for him to remember.

Jack must have dozed off while deep in thought, because an hour had passed before he knew it. He looked down at his wrist watch to check the time and it was already twelve o'clock noon. "I must hurry and get to the funeral home. I should have already been there," Jack said as he headed for the front door.

Chapter Four

Four months had passed since Wendy was cremated, and summer was here. Some of the flowers Wendy wanted Jack to plant were still in bloom. Chain was almost grown and more restless than ever. Jack didn't know what to do with Chain. He didn't want to set him free because he was afraid he wouldn't be able to fend for himself in the wild.

While looking at the flowers that he planted, Jack all of a sudden remembered the Jane Doe infant. There had been so much going on that he had completely forgotten to check on that precious little baby. "She must be about nine months old by now," Jack said, thinking out loud. "I'm going to call the welfare office today and find out whatever happened to that baby. I feel like a heel for not already asking how the baby is doing," Jack said, still thinking out loud.

Jack's thoughts were interrupted by the sound of the telephone ringing. He hurriedly walked over to the picnic table where it still lay ringing and answered it.

"Hello," Jack said into the receiver.

"Hello Jack, Ralph Conners here," Mr. Conners said.

"What can I do for you this morning?" Jack asked.

"Someone called me earlier this morning and told me that they think someone is living in that old shack about two miles south of the Thorn Place off old Highway 46. The person that called is concerned because no one has lived in that shack since old Will Shindly passed away. I want you to check this out for me," Mr. Conners replied.

"I'll get right on it, Mr. Conners. I was planning to check on the infant that Chain found last year, but I guess that can wait until later. I just wanted to find out what family has her," Jack said.

"I can save you the trouble of checking into that. Farley and Edie Winthorpe have her now. I'm not sure if they plan to adopt her or not and I'm not sure if the county has given the child a name yet. Thanks for doing this for me, Jack," Mr. Conners said as he hung up the phone.

"I wish he had given me a chance to ask him where Mr. and Mrs. Winthorpe live before he hung up the phone," Jack mumbled under his breath. Jack took the phone back inside the house and took off his good shoes and put on his old boots. After checking the caller ID for messages he might have missed, he left to check out the old shack.

As Jack was driving to the old shack, he glanced over at Chain sitting beside him. He looked as though he wanted to say that he was ready to go to work. "Are you happy to be going back to work chain?" Jack asked. "Of course you are," Jack answered for Chain.

Jack slowly applied the brakes as he approached the turn that leads to the old Will Shindly shack. As he got closer to the shack, he could see smoke coming from the chimney. There was definitely someone living there. The narrow road that led to the shack was very bumpy so Jack couldn't drive very fast. As the view of the shack became plainer, he saw a person standing in front of the cabin. Whoever it was must have seen his car, because they turned and ran around to the back of the shack.

After driving over a few more bumps Jack was finally parked in front of the old run-down shack. He silently wondered why anyone would want to live there, of all places. Jack turned off his engine, got out of the car and let Chain out of the car, put his keys in his right pants pocket, locked his door and hurriedly ran around to the back of the shack. Whoever ran must have run into the woods.

"Come on out. I'm not here to hurt you or anyone else. I only want to ask you a few questions," Jack called out to anyone who might be listening. Jack heard a rustling sound coming from the nearby trees and bushes. Chain took off into the woods before Jack could stop him, and then all of a sudden he heard a very frightened scream that sounded like the scream of a woman.

"Don't hurt me please, don't hurt me!"she screamed loud enough for people in the next county to hear her.

"Don't worry, Chain and I won't hurt you. He only wants to help you and so do I, if you will come on out so I can see you," Jack said sympathetically.

In a few seconds, a young woman stepped out from behind a large oak tree with Chain right beside her. She didn't look to be over twenty-one or twenty-two years old. She was sure in need of a good bath and some clean clothes.

"Come closer, I told you that no one is going to hurt you," Jack said reassuringly.

"Call your wolf off," the young woman said in a trembling voice.

"Come here Chain," Jack called. Chain looked up at the young woman and licked her hand and then ran toward Jack.

"Hey, he likes you," Jack laughingly said. "Let's walk back to the shack and get to know a little about each other," Jack said as he turned around to face the cabin. Jack could hear the young woman's footsteps slowly following him as he walked toward the shack while still continuing to talk to her.

"You know, it is rather peaceful out here in this neck of the woods. The sky is so blue, and the chirping of the birds aren't drowned out by the noise of trucks and cars and other annoying sounds. The trees and the wild flowers are so beautiful. Yes, I can see how a person might could get use to this kind of life," Jack said as he continued walking.

The young woman had just about caught up with Jack by the time they reached the shack. Jack turned around to see how much distance was between him and the young woman and noticed that she seemed a little calmer. He thought once he began talking to her that he would be able to put her mind at ease.

When Jack, Chain and the young woman reached the door of the shack, Jack opened the door, stood to one side so the young woman and Chain could go inside the one room shack first. Once they were inside Jack started the conversation by asking the young woman's name.

"My name is Penelope Augustine and I'm from New York. I was on my way to Florida when I was kidnaped, tied and gagged, and thrown in the back seat of my own car. I was forced to take some kind of drug and the next thing I knew I was in another car with a police officer. He said he was a police officer but I never saw a name tag. On the way here he stopped and bought groceries and told me that I would be safe here. He left and returned a few days later and raped me and told me that he would kill me if I ever left this shack. He said that he lived just a little ways from here and would know if I left. He's probably watching us right now. He will probably come and kill me after you leave," Penelope said, almost in hysterics.

"How long has that been?" Jack asked.

"It has been way over a year ago. Probably close to two years. That man got me pregnant. He brings me food out here every so often and rapes me when he feels like it. He just happened to be here when I went into labor. He delivered the baby and said that it was a little girl. I never heard her cry. He said she was dead and took her outside to his car. A few days later he said he buried her. I've tried numerous times to escape but I always see a car that looks like his and I get frightened. I tried fighting back but he's too strong for me and I only get beaten up. I would have left that first day but he said that he was going to find me a place and get me some help. I should have known better," she said in a disgusted tone of voice.

"Come on, you're getting out of here," Jack said as he took Penelope by the hand. For some reason, Jack believed every word Penelope said. "I'm so sorry that you had to go through all this," Jack said as he held the passenger door of his car open for Penelope to get in. Once Penelope was in the car Jack turned his attention to Chain. "Come here, Chain, you have to ride in the back seat this time," Jack said as he held the back door open. Chain jumped right in, as if he was trying to be a good sport about the whole situation.

"Penelope, I'm sorry I haven't already introduced myself. My name is Jack McCain and you know Chain already," Jack said apologizing for his oversight.

"That's alright. I didn't see as I had anything to lose by taking a chance with you, that is, once you called your wolf away from me. I don't even know why I ran. A helicopter was hovering over here the other day, but I don't know if they saw me. I know I rattling on and on. Anyways, it's nice to meet you, Jack, and I hope that your rescuing me doesn't get you killed," Penelope said shyly.

"Don't you worry about me. I'm a law enforcement agent, but I'm one of the good guys. My housekeeper and best friend is at my house right now and has probably got lunch almost ready. I left before she got there, but she will cook unless I call and tell her not to, and I don't know about you but I'm starved," Jack said with a little chuckle.

"Your maid won't mind me having lunch with you?" Penelope asked.

"She will just love having you for lunch. Not only will she love having you for lunch but she will just adore going shopping for you new clothes and helping you with anything that you need help with," Jack said reassuringly.

Penelope seemed content with Jack's answer and didn't say another word for the rest of the ride to Jack's house. Jack welcomed the silence because it gave him time to think. He wondered who that wicked police officer could be or if it was someone pretending to be a police officer. He had an idea and it would be a safe one for Penelope.

"This is where I live," Jack said as he turned to drive up into his driveway.

"You have a beautiful yard and house. But I didn't think to ask where do I go from here. I don't have any money and I'm sure my employer in New York has replaced me by now. My apartment and everything is history. I was just so happy to finally be leaving those woods and that shack and to have a chance at a safe life and to be free of that maniac that I didn't ask you any questions about anything," Penelope said with a little fear in her voice.

"Why don't we just get out of the car, go into the house and I'll introduce you to Mattie, my housekeeper, and we'll discuss all these other things after we eat and Mattie gets you settled.

"Something smells good and Chain, don't knock me down trying to get inside," Jack said as he opened the kitchen door while gesturing for Penelope to go in ahead of him.

"I see you have company," Mattie said while trying not to show her surprise and shock at the young woman's appearance. "Penelope, this is Mattie Wiles, and Mattie, I would like to introduce you to Penelope Augustine. Penelope has ran into some difficult times and she needs our help and understanding. Both of us are starved and something sure smells good," Jack said as he gave Mattie a "let's not embarrass the young woman anymore than we have to" look.

Mattie showed Penelope where to wash up, and while she was washing up Jack asked Mattie to go into town and buy Penelope all the clothes she would need to get a fresh start. He also told her that he would give her the money for the clothes and fill her in on everything later. When Jack and Mattie heard Penelope open the bathroom door Jack got a kitchen chair and was waiting to assist her in sitting down for lunch when she walked back into the kitchen. Mattie began setting the table as Jack motioned for Penelope to sit down.

"Thank you," Penelope said as she graciously accepted his offer and sat down. "I hope you like tuna fish casserole, crackers and homemade red velvet cake for dessert," Mattie said as she lovingly put the beautifully prepared food on the table.

"Sounds delicious," Penelope said while silently hoping that they would begin eating any second because she was starving.

"The lunch looks beautiful, so let's chow down," Jack added.

During lunch Mattie wondered what in the world happened to that seemingly-lovely young woman. She had already forgotten her name, however, she would listen and hopefully hear Jack say it and then she would write it down along with the other names that she was trying to remember. As

Mattie occasionally glanced at Penelope during lunch she thought, *behind all that disarray there's a very beautiful woman*. She decided right then and there to make a positive change in that nice young woman's life. Mattie had just taken her last bite of cake when the phone rang.

"Don't get up, Jack, I'll get it. I've finished my lunch," Mattie said as she excused herself from the table.

"It's for you, Jack," Mattie yelled from the living room while thinking that Jack needed to get a phone line installed in the kitchen. She didn't know why she hadn't already mentioned it to him or why he hadn't thought of it.

"Hello," Jack said when Mattie handed him the phone.

"Conners here. Jack, there's a fire in the apartment building on Findley drive. They need extra help," Mr. Conners said with a sense of urgency in his voice.

"I'll be right there," Jack promised.

After hanging up the phone Jack walked back into the kitchen and apologized to Penelope and Mattie for having to leave. He explained about the fire and promised to return as soon as possible. They reassured him that they understood and watched him with admiration as he headed toward the door. Chain had just finished eating and was drinking water when he heard Jack open the door to leave. He immediately turned away from his water bowl and made a beeline to Jack.

"Come on, boy. I guess it will be alright for you to go. You're smart enough to stay away from fire aren't you," Jack said as he let Chain out ahead of him.

Jack drove carefully, while hoping that no one would be hurt from the fire. Once he arrived at the now blazing building he opened the trunk of his car and took out his fireman's suit and put it on. Even though he was a volunteer firefighter, he was seldom free from his regular job to assist in much firefighting. He could feel the heat from the now blazing fire.

"Stay back, Chain," Jack ordered as he walked over to the nearest fireman to see what area he would be needed in the most. While the fireman was telling Jack how he could be of assistance, Chain headed for the burning building. With all the screaming and yelling going on, Jack didn't see Chain make a dash for the burning building. A few minutes later everyone that was standing around saw that big wonderful wolf carrying a two-year-old little boy on his back come out of the burning building. Jack could hear everyone shouting and yelling. He didn't know Chain had rescued a child until he heard someone yell out, "Hey look what that wolf just did. He just saved a child's life." Jack made his way through the crowd to see a happy mother take her child off Chain's back.

"What a wonderful animal you are," the mother happily told Chain as she turned and began to make her way through the crowd to get her child to safety.

A news reporter stopped the mother of the little boy before she could get away from the crowd and began asking questions. A fireman walked over to Jack and told him that enough volunteers showed up and that he could take Chain home. The fireman also congratulated Chain on a job well done as he excused himself to get back to work.

Jack could see the other firemen were about to get the fire under control when a reporter approached him and started asking him all kinds of questions about Chain. Jack answered her questions and asked to be excused so he could take Chain home.

Once Jack and Chain were alone in the car, Jack reached over and gave Chain the biggest hug ever. "You are one amazing animal Chain. There's so many things I want to know and you can't talk. I want to know how that little boy knew how to get on your back and how you knew that he was in that building. Oh well, I guess I don't have to know everything," Jack said while still hugging Chain.

On the ride home, Jack wondered what would have happened to that little boy if Chain hadn't been there. He wondered why the little boy was alone and if anyone else was in the building. "You would have broken your neck trying to get back in that building if anyone else was in there, wouldn't you boy?" Jack asked as he lovingly patted Chain's head. Jack felt like his heart would burst with pride during the drive home and with good reason, Jack thought. After all, Chain had risked his own life to save another life.

It was still early when Jack got home. When he opened the door to get out of the car he could smell the smoke of the burning building on himself. "Boy, you and I have got to get a bath," Jack said as Chain came bounding out of the front seat with an enormous amount of new-found energy. No sooner had Jack and Chain gotten out of the car than Mattie came running out of the house, all excited.

"What Chain did is all over the news. They had live coverage at the burning building. You must be so proud of him," Mattie said with tears of joy streaming down her face.

"You had better believe it," Jack said as he reached out and gave Mattie a big hug.

While Jack was hugging Mattie, he could see someone looking out the front door and it occurred to him that it was Penelope. "Come on out, Penelope,"

Jack called as be broke loose of his fond embrace with Mattie. He couldn't believe his eyes as Penelope slowly stepped outside with a somewhat happy look on her face.

"Doesn't she look beautiful? I just went to the nearest clothing store and bought the things she needed for right now. I wanted her to go choose the rest of her clothes," Mattie said happily.

"She certainly does look beautiful. She doesn't look like the same person," Jack replied cheerfully.

Jack watched with pleasure as Penelope slowly walked over to where he and Mattie was standing. Chain ran over to Penelope and began walking along beside her as if he were her bodyguard. Penelope's long black hair was shining and flowing beautifully with the warm soft breeze that was gently blowing. She must have been about five feet, seven inches tall and weighed about one hundred and thirty five firm pounds, which she carried very well. Her olive complexion brought out the warm color of her light brown eyes. She wasn't wearing any make-up and didn't need any. Penelope certainly did add beauty to Jack's well-groomed yard.

"You certainly look lovely, Penelope," Jack said as she slowly continued to walk closer to him and Mattie.

"Thank you. But I don't know how I will ever be able to repay you and Mattie for all that you are doing for me. Both of you have been so kind. I'm a complete stranger and you're doing all this for me," Penelope said as a lump began to form in her throat.

"Hey, what good is life if you can't help people?" Jack asked, not really expecting an answer. Penelope just smiled at Jack, and Mattie nodded her head in reply.

"Come on, let's go inside. Chain and I both need a bath. Both of us smell like smoke," Jack said as he motioned for Penelope and Mattie to move along ahead of him. When they reached the house Jack opened the door for the ladies to go inside ahead of him. Penelope was beginning to have a lot of respect for Jack. She had never had the pleasure of meeting anyone so thoughtful and kind. She was sure glad that she let him take her away from that old shack in the woods. At last she was safe and had hopes of getting her life back. She really wanted with all of her heart to someday be able to repay them for their kindness.

Jack secretly slipped Mattie enough money to pay for Penelope's clothes that she was wearing and enough to buy the rest of the things she needed as he made his way toward the bathroom.

"You ladies can finish your shopping while I take care of business here. Chain gets a bath first and then I'll get mine," Jack said as he closed the bathroom door behind him.

While the women were shopping Jack took Chain outside to the back yard and gave him a nice bath. Once Chain was clean Jack went inside and took a shower and put on clean clothes. While he was showering, he was making plans to get photographs of all the men on the payroll at work. Then he would bring them home so Penelope could look at them and then he would know if anyone he worked with was guilty of kidnaping and raping her.

After Jack finished showering and putting on fresh clean clothes he went outside and called Chain. Chain wanted to stay outside and play after getting a bath so Jack granted him that wish. Now where in the world could he be?

"Chain, come here boy!" Jack yelled. Jack continued to call out for a few more minutes when all of a sudden, Chain came leaping out of the woody area behind Jack's house.

"You need to quit running off like that, boy. Have you got a girlfriend that you're keeping hid?" Jack said as he led Chain to the car. "I've got to go to the office for a little while. Today was supposed to be my day off, but you see how that worked out. I never have an entire day off. There's always something going on," Jack said continuing to talk to Chain.

Mr. Conners wasn't in his office when Jack got there, however, he didn't think that he would mind if he ran off a copy of the recent photo that the team had made together. Everyone on the force was in the photo. Jack took the photo off the wall and out of the frame and ran a copy of it off on their office printer. Then he put the photo back in the frame and hung it back on the wall, got his copy and walked out of the office and back out to his car. Jack opened his car door and checked his front seat for poop and urine. Chain hadn't made a mess in his car in a long time but Jack wasn't about to take another chance on sitting in another pile of poop like he did once before. During the ride home Jack wonders about Penelope's past. He wonders where she worked, what kind of friends she had, if she has brothers and sisters and if her parents are still alive. Jack's thoughts wondered from Penelope. He was anxious to know what kind of a story would be in the news paper in the morning concerning Chain's rescue of the little boy.

Jack was still deep in thought when he drove up in his driveway. Mattie's car wasn't in the driveway so she and Penelope must still be shopping he thought. He got out of the car, and he and Chain went inside the house. Chain headed straight for the food bowl only to find it and his water bowl empty. Jack suddenly remembered that he had forgotten to refill them and immediately refilled both the food and water bowls. "Sorry about that, ole boy," Jack said as he put the refilled bowls back in their place. Chain lovingly licked Jack's hand and then began to chow down. Jack was walking back into the livingroom when he heard Mattie's car coming up the drive. He opened the door and walked outside to see if he could help with any packages or bags.

"Need any help, ladies?" Jack asked after opening Mattie's car door for her.

"Yes, I sure can if you don't mind," Mattie replied as she popped the trunk open. Penelope had already opened her door and got out of the car and making her way to the trunk of Mattie's car before Jack could offer to help with her door.

"I was coming around to open your door if you had only waited," Jack told Penelope as he made his way to the trunk of the car.

"That's perfectly alright. I'm not use to having anyone open doors for me," Penelope said.

"Well, let's get these packages and bags inside and then I have something to show you, Penelope," Jack said.

"I also bought a few groceries while I was in town," Mattie said as they all three retrieved the packages and bags from the trunk and made their way inside the house. Once everyone was inside the house Penelope was wondering where to put her things. She hadn't thought beyond getting out of the woods and getting to a safe place.

"What do I do with my things?" Penelope asked in wide-eyed wonder.

"Oh, you poor little darling. I guess you are lost. We've been so busy we haven't even decided where you will stay until your car can be found or you reach your family," Mattie said apologetically.

"I'm sorry, too. I didn't even think to ask you if you have family that you wish to contact. Feel free to use the phone and call anyone you need to," Jack said.

"I left home after my mother passed away. I'm an only child and my dad never cared too much for me. He wanted a son and I guess I was too much of a disappointment. I graduated high school when I was seventeen and beautician school when I was nineteen. I worked and saved my money so I could move to New York. My mom had a bad heart and dad found her dead in bed one morning. After her funeral I just didn't see any reason not to go ahead with my plans to move to New York City. Dad didn't seem to care if I stayed or left, so I left. He doesn't even know where I moved to. My mom left me a little money, so with what she left me and what I had saved I was able to get a pretty good start in New York. I guess the girls and guys I worked with think I vanished off the face of the earth. They knew I was taking a road trip to Florida, so they probably think I moved there. I don't really know what they might think; I wasn't close enough to anyone I worked with for them to be out looking for me. I have aunts, uncles, and cousins, but no one that I kept in close contact with. I'm somewhat of a loner," Penelope said, filling them in on most of her life history in a few seconds.

"I have an idea. Why doesn't Penelope come stay with me until she decides what to do?" Mattie said excitedly.

"I have an even better idea. Why don't you both stay right here until Penelope reports everything to the authorities? I should have taken pictures of her at the shack but I didn't have my camera with me. You both can sleep in the bedroom that has twin beds. Penelope will probably feel safer with another female in the room with her," Jack said, while hoping that they would agree to stay. Even though Jack liked time alone as most everyone does, he still liked having a family.

"That's fine with me if it's alright with Penelope," Mattie said cheerfully.

"Sounds good to me and I'll try not to overstay my welcome," Penelope said, agreeing with Jack and Mattie.

"Now that the sleeping arrangements are settled I have some photos that I want you to take a look at, Penelope," Jack said as he sat down on the sofa while gesturing for her to sit down beside him.

After Jack sat down and Penelope had joined him on the sofa he took out the photo that he had copied at the office. "Penelope, I want you to look at this picture and see if there is anyone in it that you recognize. If there is, then don't be afraid to tell me. I don't like anyone I work with well enough to cover up a crime for them, and what was done to you is a crime. So look very carefully and then tell me if you recognize anyone. Remember, they can't hurt you when they are behind bars and no one will hurt you while you're here," Jack said reassuringly. Penelope looked carefully and then put both hands over her face and let out a muffled scream. "That's him," she said.

"Who?" Jack asked, wondering which one of the officers she was talking about. She took her hands off her face long enough to identify Cliff Crowley.

"Man, I'll have his hide nailed to the wall. I'm so angry and I can tell you that it wouldn't do that no-good-for-nothing piece of trash to be here right now," Jack said as he jumped up from the sofa and began angrily pacing the floor.

"It's been a long day and I think we all need to calm down and get some sleep," Mattie said.

"You're right. We will all get a good night's rest and then Penelope and I will go down to the office first thing in the morning after breakfast and talk with Mr. Conners," Jack said as he headed toward his room.

"Goodnight you two, see you in the morning," Jack said as he shut the door to his room. While Jack was getting undressed and ready for bed, he was thinking how to tell Penelope that the infant that Chain found last fall might very well be her baby. He thought about telling her earlier but he didn't want to put too much on her mind at once. However, he decided to tell her after breakfast in the morning. During the ride to the office would be the perfect time.

Jack awoke early the next morning and walked outside to get the morning paper. He could hear Mattie moving around in the kitchen and he wondered if Penelope was out of bed, too. Jack took the newspaper out of the plastic bag and opened it to the front page. He ran in the house to show Mattie and Penelope that Chain's picture was on the front page, and an article about him and the little boy that he saved from the fire.

"Chain made the headlines again," Jack said as he walked into the kitchen and held up the front page so Mattie and Penelope could see Chain's picture. Chain was standing in front of the burning building.

"Read the news article out loud while Penelope and I finish breakfast," Mattie said as she put the biscuits in the oven. Jack was glad that Penelope was already out of bed so she could hear him read the article about Chain. Jack sat down at the table and began to read. The article read, "Chain: Local Hero Saves Another Life."

> "The apartment building on Findley drive was a burning inferno when a local volunteer fireman arrived with his wolf. Jack McCain found Chain when he was only a puppy and saved his little life. Now it looks as though Chain is taking the opportunity to repay that kindness by saving every life that he has a chance to save. The tenants and firemen thought everyone was out of the building. The young girl who was babysitting the young child said that he must have gone back inside to get his special toy,a stuffed rabbit. She said she only let go of his hand for a second to get something out of her purse and when she reached for his hand again he was gone. She looked at the building when she heard everyone screaming and saw the child that she was supposed to be watching on a wolf's back. The young girl says she will never again take her eyes off children who are in her care. No one was seriously

injured in the fire and the entire community thanks Chain for being so alert to the needs of others. A medal will be given to Chain for an act of bravery and kindness. We also owe thanks to Jack McCain for sharing Chain with the community."

"That is a wonderful article. I know you're very proud of Chain. I'm not as uneasy around him as I used to be and I'm very proud of him myself," Mattie said proudly.

"I certainly am proud of him," Jack said as he walked over to where Chain was eating and lovingly rubbed the top of his head.

"I only just met Chain and I'm proud to know him," Penelope said.

"Penelope, after breakfast you and I are going to take a ride to the department where I work. I want you to talk with my boss and tell him everything that you told me and I want you to file charges against Cliff Crowley for the things he did to you. I also have something to tell you on the way to the station," Jack told Penelope as he was finishing his breakfast. Jack could tell that he had gotten Penelope's and Mattie's curiosity stirred up, however neither of them said anything.

"Mattie, when I get back from the police station I will give you that new hairstyle that you and I were discussing yesterday. You are about five feet one inch tall and weigh about one hundred and ten pounds. Your hair is a lovely gray and will only need a little trimming and styling to make you absolutely gorgeous. I always look at a person's size to determine what hair style will suit them. I give my opinion and then do what the customer wants. I'm sorry, I'm just babbling on and on. I'm just so nervous and scared," Penelope said as she got up from the table to take her dishes to the sink.

"Don't be afraid Penelope, I'll be with you the entire time," Jack said reassuringly.

"You two had better get going. I'll finish up here," Mattie said while swallowing her last bite of food.

"You're right as rain, Mattie. Let's get going, Penelope," Jack said as he motioned for Penelope to follow him while heading for the door.

Once they were in the car Jack told Penelope his suspicions about the baby that Chain had found last fall in an old barn.

"Penelope, this may very well be your child, and if it is then you have the right to claim her. The child is in foster care and as far as I know she is healthy. You couldn't help what happened and if a DNA test proves that you are the mother and Cliff is the father, then I'm sure you will get your baby and Cliff will get a prison sentence," Jack said, while hoping to see a glimpse of hope in Penelope's eyes.

"You mean my baby may be alive?" Penelope said with excitement.

"I mean exactly that," Jack said as he parked the car beside Mr. Conners' at the station.

Mr. Conners was surprised to see Jack with a young lady so early in the morning. Jack introduced Penelope to Mr. Conners and told him the reason that she was in his office. Mr. Conners could see that Penelope was ashamed and assured her that she had no reason to feel ashamed.

"You have had a great injustice done to you by someone who is supposed to protect people and we will start the necessary proceedings to get the blood test to determine if the baby that was found last fall belongs to you and Cliff. We will also start an immediate investigation concerning Cliff Crowley."

Mr. Conners made all the arrangements for Penelope, the baby and Cliff to get blood test. He also put out an all points bulletin for Penelope's car, even though the odds of her getting it back were slim to none.

Chapter Five

It was now early fall and the leaves on the trees were beginning to turn a beautiful orange and yellow. It felt so good to take a deep breath of fresh air while the sun shone warmly on your face, and especially when you have just received wonderful news.

Penelope learned a few weeks before that the baby Chain found a year ago was hers and Cliff's. Cliff decided to give up all rights to his little girl if Penelope wouldn't continue to try and have him prosecuted. Penelope was so happy to have her baby that she agreed to do as Cliff wished. Cliff denied leaving the baby in the loft and said that Penelope willingly had sex with him. Everyone knew that he was lying and Jack tried to talk her into taking Cliff to court but she refused, stating that she only wanted to get on with her life and put that whole horrid mess behind her. Jack could see her point in wanting to put the past behind her, however he hated to see Cliff get away with what he had done.

Farley and Edie Winthorpe had been making plans to adopt Penelope's baby and had already given her a name. They named her Charley Alexandra. The Winthorpes hated to give Charley up; however, they realized that Penelope hadn't deserted her baby and that mother and child deserved to be together. Penelope decided to let her little girl keep the name the Winthorpes gave her since she thought it was a lovely name, and told the Winthorpes that she would keep in touch and that they could see Charley from time to time.

During Penelope's stay with Jack and Mattie, she had been able to set things right with her bank in New York. When the forged signatures didn't match Penelope's, the bank tellers tried to contact Penelope. They put a freeze on her account and after numerous failed attempts to contact Penelope they contacted the police. After going through the proper channels, Penelope was able to get her money transferred to the bank where Jack and Mattie did their banking.

There was no record that the bank in New York had ever reported anything to the police. Penelope had been missing for almost two years and there was no record anywhere that anyone had tried to find her. Jack was simply disgusted with the people who had been associated with her. It looked like someone would have reported her missing but they didn't.

Penelope now had her baby, a job working as a beautician in a large beauty salon, and her own apartment. She bought herself a good used car, and Mattie wouldn't hear of little Charley being put in day care, so she took on the responsibility of babysitting.

Everything seemed to be working out fine. Jack put his house up for sale because he wanted to move farther out in the country. The house he wanted to buy was only a few miles from where he lived and there would be more room for Chain to run and play.

Jack's sister didn't want him to sell his house because it was the house they grew up in. Their parents left it to him in their will. They left Allie a rental house just as nice, but she had sold it since she lived so far away and didn't want the responsibility of the upkeep of it. Allie and her husband Jeff were planning to visit in a few days so maybe he could talk her into seeing things his way. After all, he had been supporting that big house for over eleven years. The house he wanted to buy wasn't quite as big, had a bigger yard and more woods should he decide to take up hunting again someday.

Jack was still working with Mr. Conners on the Jim Valley case. That case was a little over a year old and still unsolved. Jack had talked with Henry Folds several times and he just knew the man was hiding something. Amanda Folds was just as strange as her father, or so it seemed. She had said she lived with her mother in Virginia. However, she seemed to have moved in with her father, because Jack saw her driving around town pretty often, at least two or three times a month.

"First thing in the morning, I'm going to surprise Mr. Folds with another visit," Jack said, thinking out loud.

"Who is Mr. Folds?" Penelope asked.

"I didn't hear you drive up. You must have already been here when I got back from the office and you wouldn't know who Mr. Folds is if I told you," replied Jack.

"I got here just shortly before you did and parked my car behind the house to keep the sun off Charley. She's taking a nap and believe me, you don't want her nap to be disturbed. She is some kind of cranky if she doesn't get to finish her nap. I just walked out here to say hello. Talk to you later. I have to check on Charley again," Penelope said as she turned to walked away.

Jack watched Penelope as she walked away. He knew he was falling in love with her and didn't know what to do about it. There was at least twelve or thirteen years' difference in their ages. She was in her early twenties and he was about to turn thirty-six. He was ready to throw Wendy's letter away, just as she had asked him to do when he fell in love again. Mattie had hopes of Jack and Dani getting together, but there just wasn't any sparks between them; or maybe they just met at the wrong time. Anyway, Jack just couldn't get Penelope out of his mind.

"Jack, someone wants you on the phone!" Mattie yelled through the open kitchen window.

"Did they say who they were?" Jack asked, yelling from the edge of the front yard.

"No they didn't, but they said that it's very important," Mattie replied.

"Tell them to hold on and I'll be right with them," Jack yelled out as he began running toward the house. Mattie met Jack halfway with the phone.

"Hello," Jack said after Mattie handed him the phone.

"Hello. This is Henry Folds. I would like for you to come to my house right away if you can," Mr. Folds said in a low, weak voice.

"I'll be there as soon as possible," replied Jack. "Mattie, I have to leave and I don't know just when I'll be home. If I'm not home in time for dinner just fix me a plate and put it in the microwave. Tell Penelope I'll talk to her later," Jack said as handed the phone back to Mattie.

"Penelope left right before the phone rang a few minutes ago. You must not have heard her leave," Mattie replied.

"I probably didn't, I've had a lot on my mind lately," Jack said as he turned to walk toward his car.

On the ride to Mr. Folds' house, Jack was wondering what in the world was so important that Mr. Folds wanted him to come to his house right away. All of a sudden, his train of thought shifted from Mr. Folds to Chain. He hadn't checked on Chain before he left. Chain usually heard Jack when he opened the house doors or the car doors. "Maybe Chain was just busy eating and didn't hear me leave," Jack thought as he parked his car in front of Mr. Folds house.

Mr. Folds was sitting in the living room in his recliner when Jack arrived at his house. He had purposely left the front door to his house open. When Mr. Folds heard Jack walk toward the door he called out for him to come on in.

Jack opened the door and stepped inside. He took one look at Mr. Folds and knew that he was a sick man.

"You don't look well, Mr. Folds. Let me drive you to the hospital or to your doctor's office, whichever you prefer," Jack said in a sympathetic voice.

"There's no need for that. There's nothing that can be done. I'm dying and I want to die at home. Read this, it explains everything. I'm too weak to talk," Mr. Folds said as he handed him a stuffed envelope. Jack opened the envelope and unfolded the letter. He was completely dumfounded when he realized that this letter was a confession to a murder. After sitting down in a chair next to Mr. Folds, Jack began to silently read the confession. Mr. Folds must have written the confession sometime earlier, because he appeared to be too weak to do much writing now.

The confession read:

To Whom It May Concern,

I, Henry Folds being of sound mind, confess to the murder of Jim Valley. He had tried to sell drugs to someone that I love very much. I wanted to make sure that he didn't sell them to anyone else. I knew that no one could prove that Ralph Conners committed the crime. I don't even know why I tried to implicate Ralph. I knew that I was dying and I would have come forward before I let someone else take the wrap for something I did. I know that I was wrong for doing what I did, however there is one consolation and that is Jim Valley won't sell or give drugs to anyone else. I called Jim Valley the day I killed him and asked him to meet me at the barn near the water tower on old Highway 46. Jim was drinking pretty heavily and did cocaine right in front of me. If he hadn't passed out I probably wouldn't have been able to smother him, but he made it all too easy. No one else knows anything about this terrible crime I committed.

Jack could hardly believe what he just read.

"Mr. Folds why didn't you tell me all this before now?" Jack asked in wonderment.

"I think the reasons are obvious. I didn't want to go to prison because of a drug pusher. I'm not trying to condone what I did, I'm only telling you why," Mr. Folds said in a weak voice.

"I'll take care of this for you. I must leave now, but before I go I'll call someone to come sit with you until you feel stronger," Jack said in an understanding voice.

"That's alright. I would really like to be alone for a little while. You go do whatever it is that you have to do," Mr. Folds said as he closed his eyes again. Mr. Folds appeared to be asleep, so Jack stood up and quietly left. Jack put Mr. Folds' confession in his glove compartment once he was seated in his car. He knew he had to show the confession to Mr. Conners as soon as possible. However, the first thing he had to do was to go by his house and check on Chain.

During the ride home Jack wondered if Jim Valley had tried to sell Amanda drugs. That was the only person he knew of that Mr. Folds could have gotten that angry over. The confession didn't say what reason Mr. Folds gave for wanting to meet with Jim. Mr. Folds was too weak to answer a lot of questions, so Mr. Conners would have to make the decision on how to close the case with the evidence that they had.

Jack was still trying to understand what happened to cause Mr. Folds to snap. Maybe Mr. Folds didn't even know. Sometimes a lot of things can happen to a person, and then one day something can happen to cause that person to snap. Maybe that's what had happened to Mr. Folds. Maybe his years as a police officer affected him in a negative way. Jack was still deep in thought when he parked his car in his drive.

Chain came running out to meet Jack as soon as he heard him drive up in the driveway. Jack could tell from the mud on Chain's paws that he had been fooling around in the woods again. "Chain ole pal, I do believe you're keeping secrets from me. I believe you have a girlfriend that you're keeping hidden," Jack said as he bent down and picked up a stick to throw for Chain to fetch.

"Mattie, I'm home," Jack called out as he opened the back door.

"Good, I was just getting ready to write you a note telling you that someone called and wants to look at the house. I took the liberty of telling them that they can come tomorrow around noon. You're usually home for lunch around that time. If you're not, then I can show them the house, if that's alright with you," Mattie exclaimed as she joined Jack in the kitchen.

"That sounds good to me. I may have to work through lunch tomorrow. There's a lot going on at work right now. If I should have to work through lunch I would appreciate it tremendously if you would show the house for me," Jack said in a strained voice.

"Are you alright ?" Mattie asked in a very concerned tone of voice.

"I'm just mentally exhausted, but I'll be fine," Jack replied.

"If you don't need me for anything, then I will see you tomorrow. I'm going over to Penelope's for a while so she can style my hair again," Mattie said as she picked up her purse off the kitchen table.

"You go ahead with your plans. I'm fine. And by the way I'm glad you and Penelope are such good friends," Jack replied.

"Thanks and by the way, Will Simon is the one who wants to look at your house," Mattie said as she opened the door to leave.

"That's great. He's Chain's vet. Maybe I'll get to be here when he comes to look at the house," Jack said as he opened the fridge to get a bottle of water.

"That's right, I've heard you speak of Will Simon. Well, see you tomorrow," Mattie said as she closed the door behind her. Mattie was anxious to leave to go to Penelope's. She had really enjoyed helping Penelope with little Charley and Penelope showed her appreciation by doing nice things for Mattie as often as she could.

Jack was still thinking about how nice it was that Mattie and Penelope were friends when his thoughts were interrupted by Chain nudging the back of his leg with his nose. "I guess you're hungry, fellow," Jack said as he opened the pantry door to take out the dog food.

After Chain finished eating Jack took him outside and hosed off his feet and brushed his hair. "I can't take you to see Mr. Conners looking all dirty and messy. I also have to clean up the dirt and mess that you tracked into the house. Mattie must not have noticed it or else she would have had our hides," Jack jokingly told Chain.

Mr. Conners was sitting at his desk, going through some papers when Jack and Chain walked into his office. He looked up when he heard Jack open his office door.

"Did you hear the latest?" Mr. Conners asked Jack.

"What are you talking about?" Jack asked in reply.

"A young girl called an ambulance to 333 Cleveland Avenue. Apparently the girl found her father lying on the living room floor, barely breathing. The man is Henry Folds. I knew him a long time ago. I didn't even know he was living here. People use to say that we looked like twins. We even did a background check to see if we were related. Turned out that we were just look alikes, no blood relations whatsoever. We didn't keep in touch so I don't know anything about what has been going on with him," replied Mr. Conners.

"Will you excuse me for a moment?" Jack asked as he turned to leave. "I'll be right back," he added.

"What in the world has gotten into him?" Mr. Conners mumbled to himself as he watched Jack walk away.

Jack was only gone for a minute or so and was surprised to see that Chain hadn't followed him when he walked out to his car to get Mr. Folds' written confession.

"What's that in your hand?" Mr. Conners asked when he saw Jack walk back into his office holding an envelope.

"You need to read this," Jack said as he handed the envelope to Mr. Conners. Mr. Conners opened the envelope and took out the confession and silently read it.

"What the…,"Mr. Conners said as he looked up with the most confused look that Jack had ever seen on anyone's face.

"I can't explain it myself. Mr. Folds seemed to be a very confused man. It's obvious now that he was a very disturbed man. He has a daughter named Amanda and I've seen her riding around town several times during this past year," Jack said.

"What did he mean that no one would believe that I killed Jim Valley?" Mr. Conners asked. "I didn't know I was a suspect," he added.

"Let me see if I can shed some light on this whole mess," Jack told Mr. Conners as he sat down in a chair facing Mr. Conners' desk.

"Please do just that!" Mr. Conners exclaimed.

"You and I and the rest of the team in this office are drug investigators and I do a lot of undercover work. Am I right so far?" Jack said, trying to explain.

"You're right so far, but quit beating around the bush and get on with it," Mr. Conners replied.

"I knew that the homicide department was handling the investigation, but I had a little investigating to do own my own. Mr. Folds called me after we found Jim Valley's body and wanted to meet me. He said that he had some news about Jim Valley's death. Something about knowing who killed him. I guess he was trying to get the heat off himself in case someone saw him. I don't know his real reason. Anyway, we made an appointment to meet but he didn't show up. Instead, he sent his daughter Amanda. She wasn't a lot of help. Later, Cliff Crowley said that you were having an affair with Candy Valley. He thought that I already knew, but I didn't. Anyway the description that was given to me of the murderer fit you, but it also fit Mr. Folds. I didn't tell you because I didn't really have anything to tell other than hunches, or so I thought at the time. Now that I look back I can see that I should have confided in you," Jack said.

"You certainly should have. My relationship with Candy is very complicated and has been from the very beginning. I was investigating her husband and through chance meetings we gradually fell in love. But I wasn't having an affair with her like everyone thought. People form opinions too quickly and that causes a lot of misunderstandings. Don't you keep anything else like this from me again. If I wanted to I could have your badge for withholding evidence like this from me, but I won't this time. But you had better never let anything like this happen again," Mr. Conners said as his conversation was interrupted by the ringing of the phone. The phone quit ringing before Mr. Conners could answer it.

"Must have been a wrong number," Jack said.

"Probably so," said Mr. Conners in reply.

"Well, getting back to where we left off, I was just talking to Mr. Folds no more than a couple of hours ago and I offered to take him to the hospital or to his doctor's office. I offered to call someone to come sit with him, but he said that he wanted to die at home and that he wanted to be alone for a while. I was planning to check in on him a little later. I think you and I need to go to the hospital and check on Mr. Folds and his condition," Jack said as he stood up ready to go.

"You're right. But first let me inform the fellow officers where I'll be," replied Mr. Conners. "You realize that I have to turn all this evidence over to the homicide department." Mr. Conners told Jack as they got in the car to drive to the hospital.

"I know. That's why I gave you Mr. Folds' written confession. I knew that you would know how to handle it. Since Mr. Folds named you in his confession I thought that you should be the first one to see it," replied Jack. Mr. Conners just nodded his head in agreement as he closed the car door.

"I guess Henry was just trying to keep the heat off of himself for a little while in case someone saw him, but I don't appreciate him trying to implicate me," Mr. Conners said in disgust.

"You never know what a desperate and confused person will do," replied Jack.

Jack and Mr. Conners rode in silence all the way to the hospital. Jack felt bad about not confiding in Mr. Conners, however, he thought he was doing the right thing at the time. There had been so much going on in his life since Jim Valley was murdered that he seemed to be walking around in a daze half of the time. Maybe that was why Mr. Conners was being so easy on him.

By the time Jack and Mr. Conners arrived at the hospital, Mr. Folds had passed away. His daughter Amanda was in the emergency room talking to Will Simon. She recognized Jack right away and motioned for him to join her and Will. Jack whispered to Mr. Conners what was going on and asked to be excused and told him that he would introduce him to Amanda in a few minutes. Amanda informed Jack that her father had died. She introduced Will Simon as her fiancée and informed him that Will wanted to buy his house.

"Mattie told me that Will called and wanted to look at my house tomorrow. Maybe I can be home when you come tomorrow, Will," Jack said as he shook Will's hand.

"I hope so," replied Will.

"My father was a very sick man, physically and emotionally. I would go over to his house and try to get him to confide in me and he wouldn't. He would just tell me that he wanted to be left alone, that he had a lot on his mind. He had a very bad heart condition and he became very depressed when he had to quit work. I know I told you all about this the last time we talked," Amanda said while turning to look at Will as if to get some sort of approval for her having a conversation with another man.

"I knew Amanda's father and so did Mr. Conners, years ago," Jack told Will as he motioned for Mr. Conners to come join in their conversation.

After talking with Amanda, Mr. Conners felt better about Mr. Folds. He didn't condone what Mr. Folds did but he figured that Mr. Folds must have been trying to protect Amanda. He knew that he had to turn all the information over to homicide and let them close the case.

Jack and Mr. Conners told Amanda if there was anything that either of them could do to help not to hesitate to call them. They also congratulated her and Will on their upcoming marriage. On the way back to the office they discussed what a hard time Amanda must have been through with her father. Jack told Mr. Conners that he was glad the case was finally solved and that as soon as he dropped him off at the office he had to take Chain home.

Before Jack left to take Chain home, Mr. Conners informed him that he had gotten some new information earlier in the day concerning Jim Valley's contacts, and as soon as he had more to go on that he would be calling him.

Chapter Six

Seven months have passed and it was spring again. The flowers were in full bloom, the leaves on the trees were green and the air smelled of honeysuckles.

Jack sold his house to Will Simon and moved farther out into the country. Now Chain had more room to run and play. Jack's new house was white with blue trim. The yard was blessed with beautiful oak and elm trees and lots of flowers. Even though Jack was in love with Penelope, he still remembered Wendy with love, especially in springtime

Will and Amanda got married in December and were now expecting their first child. Amanda got news that her mother met and married a wealthy land developer and that they were going to tour Italy on their honeymoon. Mr. Folds left his home and a five hundred thousand dollar life insurance policy to Amanda. She still didn't know that her father killed Jim Valley. Somehow, it didn't make the news and no one ever told her.

Cliff Crowley hadn't been seen around town since Penelope agreed not to try and prosecute him. However, Cliff was put on suspension and was still being investigated concerning his actions with Penelope and not reporting the birth of his daughter.

When Jack told Penelope that he loved her she broke down and cried. She told him that she loved him too and that their age difference didn't matter to her.

Jack had been investigating the leads that Mr. Conners gave him shortly after Mr. Folds died. He planned on being able to bust up that drug ring shortly, with a little help.

Mattie still baby sits little Charley and keeps house for Jack. Jack thinks that Chain may have a female wolf companion that he visits in the woods, because he is more restless than ever.

"Jack, someone wants you on the telephone!" Mattie yell from the kitchen.

"I'll get it in the bedroom," Jack replied sleepily. "Mattie's here early this morning," Jack thinks to himself as he answers the phone.

"Hello, this is Jack McCain," Jack said with a note of curiosity in his voice.

"Ralph Conners here. Jack, I need you to meet me at the hospital. There's a young boy who's has just been admitted due to a drug overdose. I can tell that I woke you up, so get your clothes on and meet me at the hospital," said Mr. Conners.

Jack hurriedly got out of bed and put his clothes on without even taking a shower. He brushed his teeth and ran for the back door while telling Mattie that he would grab a bite to eat later as he ran out the door.

"That poor thing is always in a hurry. He's going to get sick if he doesn't slow down. That wolf of his runs just as much as he does. Both of them are always on the run," Mattie mumbled to herself as she watched Jack hurrying out to his car. She saw Chain make a dash for the car, almost knocking Jack down as he jumped in the car first. "That big ole wolf is going to hurt Jack one of these days, trying to get in the car first. Jack doesn't get the car door open good until Chain is pushing is way into the car," Mattie said, continuing to mumble to herself.

Mr. Conners was waiting for Jack at the emergency room door, all excited. "I'm telling you, Jack, we have got to put a stop to these drugs. That young boy is only fourteen years old. I hope that child lives and doesn't suffer any brain damage and I hope he remembers who gave him those stinking drugs," Mr. Conners said angrily as he ushered Jack into the emergency room.

"It's a terrible thing for anyone to overdose on drugs, but it's just worse when it's a young person. They risk throwing their whole life away to try something that is only going to kill them sooner or later," Jack said as he noticed a young girl standing near the receptionist desk. He could see that she had been crying and he overheard her ask the receptionist on duty if she could see her little brother. No sooner had she asked than a woman came out from the back where they keep the emergency patients, crying her heart out.

Jack and Mr. Conners learned that the little boy didn't make it. The drugs were just too much for his young body. He never regained consciousness, so he couldn't tell who gave him the drugs. Jack and Mr. Conners talked with the young boy's mother and told her how sorry they were that her little boy had died and that they were going to do everything in their power to put an end to the drug problem in their community. Even though they knew that wasn't much comfort to her, they meant every word of it. They learned that the little boy's mother had found him early that morning lying on his bedroom floor and his window was open. She said that she had checked on him the night before around ten o'clock before going to bed herself and that he was in bed and appeared to be asleep. They expressed their regrets to the little boy's mother once more and then excused themselves.

"I'll meet you back at the office," Mr. Conners told Jack as they walked out of the emergency room together.

During the ride back to the office Jack wondered what that poor mother must be going through. She had checked on her son before she went to bed and thought he was safe. The sad thing was that the child was capable of hiding the fact that he was a drug addict until it was too late for him to get help. Parents work, support their children financially and try their best to protect them from harm and then something like this happens. *Sometimes this job is just too much for me*, Jack thought as he parked his car in the office parking lot.

"Come on Chain, let's go inside while I go over some reports. You've sat in the car long enough. But first, go over there and visit those bushes before you go inside. I'll wait right here for you," Jack said while watching Chain obediently do as he was told.

Mr. Conners was already at the office and sitting at his desk when Jack got there. Jack stopped by Mr. Conners' office before going to his own office to see if he needed to get any new addresses. Mr. Conners gave him a list of names and addresses of suspects that he wanted him to check out. He also told him to call him at the office or wherever he may be before checking those addresses out or making a bust so he could have back-up standing by. Jack promised that he would do exactly as Mr. Conners asked.

When Jack finished talking with Mr. Conners he decided that he didn't need to go into his office after all. Everything he needed for his job was either in his car or at his house. "Come on Chain, let's go to the house," Jack said as he held the door open for Chain.

Jack could see Mattie running away from the edge of the yard toward the side door of the house like she was running for her life as he was driving up into his driveway.

"Something must have really frightened her," Jack said to himself as he parked the car. He didn't even take time to take his keys out of the ignition. He just told Chain to get out of the car as he ran to check on Mattie. Mattie had already made it inside the house and was at the kitchen sink, getting herself a glass of water before Jack even made it to the door.

"Mattie, where are you?" Jack yelled out as he opened the side door and ran into the house and in the direction of the kitchen.

"I'm in the kitchen, getting myself a glass of water," Mattie replied sounding as though she were about to pass out from exhaustion.

"What were you running from?" Jack asked in a frightened tone of voice.

"I saw a man coming toward the house while I was at the edge of the yard feeding the squirrels. Then a big white wolf came out of nowhere and started running toward the man. That man looked like Cliff Crowley. I got so scared that I thought I would die. You know I'm not as young as I used to be," Mattie said.

"A person wouldn't know that by watching you run. But I'm sure glad that you are able to run and you did the right thing by running too," Jack told Mattie as he took hold of her wrist to check her pulse.

"Do you suppose that was Cliff Crowley?" Mattie asked Jack as he continued to check her pulse.

"If it was, then he is certainly up to no good. Law enforcement agents like him make it hard on the good ones. You can't blame people for distrusting the law when there's scum like that working as law enforcers. We get them off the force when we find out that they're crooked, but look at the damage they do in the meantime," Jack replied.

"Is my pulse alright?" Mattie asked as Jack let go of her arm.

"You'll be here forever," Jack said as he lightly patted Mattie on her shoulder.

"Many more scares like the one I just got and I won't be," Mattie said as she got herself another glass of water.

"Mattie, I'm going to call Penelope and tell her to put her and Charley some clothes in a bag and come over here for a few days. If that was Cliff in the woods then he's probably going to be afraid to come around here for awhile. He may be injured and if he is then it serves him right for fooling around where he doesn't belong. That wolf is probably a female and more than likely followed us from the old house. If she has pups then that's why she got after Cliff. She won't harm us because she knows that we live here," Jack said just before he picked up the phone to call Penelope.

"Thank goodness you're at home," Jack said when Penelope answered the phone.

"What's the matter?" Penelope asked, sounding worried.

"I'll tell you when you get here. Just get yourself and little Charley some clothes in a bag and come on over. I'll explain everything when you get here," said Cliff.

"I can tell that you're serious, so I'll do as you say," said Penelope.

"Mattie and I will be waiting for you," Jack said as he hung up the phone.

"You don't have to worry about that wolf hurting me, because there's no way that I'm going out to the edge of that yard unless you're outside close by," Mattie said as Jack hung up the phone with Penelope.

"I told you, that wolf won't hurt you. She knows that you aren't going to hurt her or her pups if she has any. She has probably been eating the table scraps that you throw out ever since I moved here and considers you a friend. Who knows, she may have only been protecting you. She knew that Cliff Crowley or whoever the man was didn't live here and she took care of him for you," Jack said, trying to convince Mattie not to be afraid.

It took Penelope only forty-five minutes to pack and get to Jack's house. Jack was outside with Chain when she arrived. Mattie was standing at the back door looking out at Jack and Chain. She was concerned about their safety.

"Penelope, you and Charley go inside. Just leave your bags and I'll bring them in later. I'll be in shortly and explain everything to you," Jack called out as he saw Penelope get out of her car.

As soon as Jack was sure that Penelope and Charley were safely in the house, he began a search in the woods near his house. As he walked farther into the woods he could see some blood on some leaves. He reached into his pocket for a plastic bag and realized that he had forgotten to get any more bags. "I'll just have to carry the bloody leaves in my hands and try not to get any blood on myself," Jack said, thinking out loud.

While Jack was in the woods searching for evidence, Mattie was filling Penelope in on everything that had been going on.

Only a few seconds after finding the bloody leaves, Chain walked up to Jack carrying in his mouth what looked to be part of a back pocket of a pair of pants. Jack took the blue jean material out of Chain's mouth to inspect it for blood and saw a few specks of what looked like blood. Jack and Chain looked around for a few more minutes and then Jack decided that Cliff or whoever had been in the woods was probably long gone by now and somewhere nursing their wounds.

"Let's go back to the house, boy. I need to get this evidence in a bag and take it to the crime lab to see if the blood on it matches Cliff's. I'm glad we have his blood type and DNA on file," Jack said as he stroked the top of Chain's head with his empty hand. Just as Jack and Chain turned to walk back to the house, a big white wolf appeared in the distance, about fifty feet to the right of them.

"That must be the white wolf that Mattie saw," Jack said to himself as he watched Chain go running to meet the other wolf. Jack learned in only a few seconds that the white wolf was a female and apparently a new mother. "Chain must be the father of those pups," Jack thought to himself as he once again made his way toward the house. "Chain, my man, come on to the house when you've finished courting. If you want to ride with me then you had better get a move on," Jack laughingly said as he continued walking toward the house.

Jack could see Mattie and Penelope looking out the kitchen window as he approached the house. He was only about twenty feet from the house when both the women and little Charley came running out the kitchen door to see if he was alright. Penelope grabbed him from one side and Mattie from the other and little Charley grabbed a leg. "Be careful, you three, I'm carrying bloody evidence in my hands and I don't want to mess it up. Besides, I'm sure you don't want to get any germs that might be on it," Jack said as he bent down to give Charley a kiss on the cheek. "How's my best girl?" Jack asked as he kissed Charley and then turned to give her beautiful mother a kiss.

"We're both fine. But what the three of us want to know is how are you and what did you find?" Penelope replied with wide-eyed curiosity.

"That's right," Mattie agreed. "Let's go inside so I can put my findings in a plastic bag and then I'll answer all of your questions," Jack said lovingly as he shooed the women and little Charley in the direction of the house. Once inside the house, Jack got a plastic bag and put his new-found evidence in it. Then he explained everything that had happened while he was searching in the woods.

"While I'm gone to the lab I want you two to stay in the house. I'm going to call Chain inside before I leave, and he will let you know if anyone is prowling around outside. I do believe he could hear a pin drop from a mile away," Jack said as he opened the kitchen door to yell for Chain.

"Do you think that blood could be Cliff's?" Penelope asked Jack as she watched him waiting for Chain to come to the house.

"It's very possible. Mattie has seen Cliff enough from time to time to recognize him when she sees him. Anyway, don't either of you open that door for anyone while I'm gone," Jack said in a concerned tone of voice.

Jack stood at the kitchen door and yelled for Chain for what seemed to be thirty minutes when finally Chain came running toward the house with the white wolf following. Chain didn't stop until he reached the house, but the white wolf stopped at the edge of the woods and then, once Chain was in the house, she turned and ran back into the woods. Once Chain was inside the house he turned and looked out the opened kitchen door and let out a mournful howl which sent cold chills through Jack, Mattie, and Penelope.

"That poor thing is just not happy living like a human. He wants to be wild as he was intended to be," said Mattie.

"I know he wants to be free, but I'm not sure if he could manage on his own. I'm going to have to give that a lot more thought," Jack said as he nudged Chain away from the door.

"You two do as I said and don't let anyone in while I'm gone. If Chain starts behaving like someone is outside, then immediately call me and I'll come home right away," Jack said as he squeezed himself through the slightly opened kitchen door to leave. Once Jack was outside he closed the door, then turned the doorknob to be sure the door was locked. *The sooner I get this business over with, the better I'll feel about Penelope and Charley going outside*, Jack thought to himself as he got in his car to leave.

While Jack was driving to the office, he silently wondered why Cliff would be prowling around his house. He truly hoped that he wasn't wanting to harm Penelope, Charley or Mattie. Whatever his reasons were Jack was sure that he was up to no good.

Once inside the crime lab Jack went immediately to the person in charge and explained the importance of the test that needed to be done on the evidence that he was labeling in their presence. The person in charge assured Jack that they would do the necessary test as soon as possible and then forward the report to the proper department.

Jack drove straight to Mr. Conners office after leaving the crime lab. Mr. Conners was walking out of the office building as Jack parked his car.

"Wait up!" Jack yelled as he ran to catch Mr. Conners before he got in his car to leave.

"What's up?" Mr. Conners asked as he turned around to face Jack.

"I need to talk with you about something that just happened," replied Jack. Jack explained everything that had happened since he had left the office earlier that morning. Mr. Conners told Jack that someone called the Sheriff's department earlier and reported seeing a bloody man running out of the woods as they were coming into town. The area they reported seeing the man wasn't far from Jack's house. The sheriff's department and the police were on the look out for a person fitting the description that the caller gave. Mr. Conners got a call while he was talking to Jack telling him that a deputy from the sheriff's department had found the bloody man near the city limits. The deputy called an ambulance and the man is now in the emergency room getting medical attention.

"Let's go to the emergency room, Jack. I do believe your prowler has been apprehended. At least he is where you can identify him from the description that Mattie gave you. We can have Mattie come in later and identify him if we need to," Mr. Conners told Jack as he gestured for him to ride with him in his car to the hospital.

"Talk to me, Mr. Conners, and remind me that I need to be a professional," Jack said nervously.

"You'll be fine Jack. You are a professional. Just remind yourself that Penelope and Charley are safe and we will cross all our bridges when we get to them," Mr. Conners assured Jack.

When Jack and Mr. Conners got to the emergency room Mr. Conners told the head nurse that he and Jack needed to see the patient who was brought in by ambulance a few minutes earlier. Since there had only been one brought in by ambulance in the past two hours Mr. Conners didn't have to do any more explaining. Jack stood still and took a deep breath before walking back to the patient area. The nurse gestured toward the cubicle that the patient they were looking for was in.

When Jack saw that the patient was Cliff Crowley, he became filled with anger. Mr. Conners watched with admiration as he saw how Jack was able to calm himself down in a situation that a lot of people might not have been able to use self control, including himself.

"Cliff, don't say a word until I finish saying what I have to say. Then the deputy who is waiting outside will read you your rights and then ask you what you were doing on my land, behind my house, before you were attacked by a wolf. I found blood on some leaves and a blue jeans pants pocket with what looked like blood on it. The leaves and pants pocket are at the crime lab right now being tested to see if the blood matches your blood. Remember, don't say anything until you have had you rights read to you. And remember, you have the right to have an attorney present," Jack said in a shaky voice.

"Man, I don't need an attorney. I only hoped to get a glimpse of my little girl. I admit to putting her in the hay loft the day I delivered her. My intentions were to sell her and get the money to start a new life in a new town. But my life hasn't been worth one red cent since I kidnaped Penelope. I've watched from a distance at the life Penelope and my little girl have with you. The more I watch, the more I hate my life. I know I can never have my baby or Penelope, but maybe by admitting and paying for my crime I can start my life over with peace of mind," Cliff said.

"Man, you're making the right decision," Mr. Conners replied as he watched Jack turn around and walk away from Cliff's bedside without saying a word. Mr. Conners followed him after he got the deputy to come and read Cliff his rights. Cliff then gave another confession to the deputy in Mr. Conners' presence.

Jack left the emergency room and walked outside to the parking lot. Mr. Conners joined him a few minutes later.

"Why did you just walk out like that, man?" Mr. Conners asked Jack as he walked toward him in the emergency room parking lot.

"I don't know. You think you've got a person figured out, and then they go and do something like that. Just like Mr. Folds. I thought he was identifying you as Jim Valley's killer and the whole time he was just trying to keep anyone from suspecting him just in case an eye witness came forward. Then he blows my mind with a written confession. You never know what to expect from people," replied Jack as he wiped his forehead with his handkerchief.

"Yeah, I know. But you must have been relieved when you heard him confess," Mr. Conners said, trying to ease Jack's mind. "I just can't believe that he has turned over a new leaf that quick. He just may be up to something. Maybe he has changed, maybe not, I don't know; but I'm not ready to believe him just yet," Jack said as he waited for Mr. Conners to unlock the doors so he could get in the car.

During the ride back to the office, Jack thought about Penelope and Charley. He made up his mind to ask her to marry him. Even though Cliff wasn't a person to be trusted, he got Jack to thinking how it must feel to be on the outside looking in on a dream that will never come true for you. He knew he loved Penelope and Charley, and he didn't want to lose them. The thought of marriage had always made Jack uneasy. He was afraid that he wouldn't be a good husband, and not only did he have to worry about being a good husband but he also had to worry about being a good father.

In the short time it took to get from the hospital to the office, Jack had the next month of his personal life all planned. He wanted Mattie to make a nice candle light dinner next Saturday at his house and then watch Charley so that he could propose to Penelope. After all, they would be spending the rest of their lives together in that house, so why not start if off with proposing marriage there. Jack had really grown to like and respect Mr. Conners, so he thought he would ask him to be his best man. He hoped that his sister Allie's feelings wouldn't be hurt by him not asking her husband Jeff to be best man, but he and Jeff hadn't ever had the opportunity to get to really know each other.

Chapter Seven

Mr. Conners was surprised yet happy that Jack wanted him to be his best man. Mattie was more than happy to plan and make a candle light dinner and babysit Charley. Mattie confessed to Jack that she had really had her heart set on him and her niece Dani getting married someday, but she knew now that they wouldn't have been happy together.

Jack called his sister Allie and invited her and Jeff to his wedding. He really hoped after all this planning that Penelope wouldn't say no when he asked her to marry him. It would be May in a couple of weeks, and that seemed like a good time to get married. They could do everything right there at the place where they would be living and raising their family. Now, all Jack had to do was to pick up the phone and call Penelope and ask her to come over for dinner. He knew that he shouldn't be nervous, but he was.

"Good morning, sweetheart," Jack said when Penelope answered the phone.

"Good morning to you, too," Penelope pleasantly replied.

"How would you like to come have dinner at my place tonight? Mattie has agreed to watch Charley for us," Jack said, while secretly hoping that she hadn't made other plans.

"Sounds wonderful to me. Is there anything that you want me to bring?" Penelope asked. "Just your beautiful self. I need to go now and I'll pick you up at seven, if that's alright," Jack said, while feeling light-headed with happiness.

"That's fine with me. Bye now," Penelope said, as she hung up the phone.

When Jack hung up the phone with Penelope, he sat down at the kitchen table and talked to Mattie while she made plans for his and Penelope's dinner. He apologized to Mattie for asking her to make a candlelight dinner on such short notice. She assured him that it was alright and that she was more than happy to do it. They also talked about the white wolf and the puppies that hadn't been seen running around yet. Of course, it had only been a few days since they had seen the white wolf and she may have only just had the pups. Mattie revealed her fears about Cliff and the possibility of him someday causing trouble for Jack and Penelope. She also told Jack of her fear of those pups growing up and maybe attacking Charley someday. Mattie was also concerned about Jack getting hurt during the investigations that he had been doing recently. Even though he hadn't discussed the investigations with her, she still knew when he was on a case.

Jack tried to reassure Mattie that Cliff would be in jail for awhile, and that he had been ordered to get counseling while in jail. He also told her that he and Penelope would be informed prior to Cliff's parole and that they weren't going to worry about Cliff until then. Mattie and her fear of animals were a hopeless case. Try as he might, Jack couldn't convince her that most wild animals only attacked if they or their young ones were in danger. And Mattie should have known by now that he was very careful while investigating leads, and he hoped to wrap up the case that he was working on pretty soon.

It was still early in the morning and Jack had promised Mr. Conners that he would check on those leads again. He would take Chain this time, and maybe he would be able to find out if any drugs were in that old building near the railroad tracks and car wash on the outskirts of town.

"Mattie, I'll be back in time to take a bath and get ready for dinner," Jack said as he got up to leave.

"Don't forget that you told Penelope that you would pick her up at seven. And please be careful," Mattie said with an unmistakable note of concern in her voice.

"Don't worry; I will," Jack said. Jack was just getting ready to open the kitchen door and yell for Chain when he saw him through the window running away from the woods toward the house.

"Come here, boy," Jack said as he opened the kitchen door to let him in. "Did you feed Chain this morning?" Jack asked Mattie.

"Yes I did. His outside food and water bowl were empty so I filled them.

I know that you only fill the inside bowls if you plan to make him stay inside," replied Mattie.

"That's good. Since he's already eaten we can leave for the office immediately," Jack said he ushered Chain back outside. "Come on boy, let's go to work," Jack told Chain as he headed toward the car.

All Jack had to do when he got to the office was pick up the clothes that he would be wearing. This time, he will be dressing as an old lady.

"Have you got my disguise?" Jack asked Mr. Conners as he entered his office.

"It's right over there, in that bag beside the water cooler. You'll be checking things out dressed as an old lady. Some people like to put clothes on their pets, so I took the liberty of buying Chain a hat and a dog coat. I guess it's a dog coat, or it's whatever you want to call it. Chain is somewhat of a celebrity and if you don't dress him up, too, then he might be recognized. After all, you don't see a wolf that often," Mr. Conners replied while trying not to laugh.

"Well if we make a drug bust today, it will be because the drug dealers died laughing. So will everyone else who sees us," Jack said, trying not to laugh himself.

"You may have a point. Anyway go to the Sunshine Palace to room 34 and park your car next door at the donut shop. There's a nice older model pink Cadillac parked right in front of room 34 and that's the car that you will be driving. When you get to that old building and anyone asks you what or who you are looking for then you tell them that you are suppose to pick up your maid there. Act like you're really senile and in that get-up you won't have any trouble playing the part. If there's any drugs there then Chain will let you know and there will be a back-up team in an old van nearby that will hear everything that's going on because you and Chain will be wired. That's one more reason for the dog coat," Mr. Conners said as he handed Jack the motel and Cadillac key. "By the way Jack, there will be an agent there waiting for you in the motel room. She will help get you and Chain wired," Mr. Conners added.

"Chain's waiting in the car. I sure hope I don't have a problem getting him to wear a hat and coat," Jack said as he picked up the bag of clothes and turned to leave. "You can talk him into it. You can get that wolf to do anything," Mr. Conners said as he watched Jack walk away.

"Boy, you aren't going to like these plans at all," Jack told Chain as he got in his car to leave. Chain just gave Jack an innocent look as though to say, I trust you. Chain always did have a way of looking at Jack and making him feel bad at just the right moment.

"The pink Cadillac is parked right where Mr. Conners said it would be. Now to get this dressing part over with," Jack thought as he parked his car in the donut shop parking lot. "I sure hope we're not recognized by anyone," Jack said to Chain as they were walking to the Sunshine Palace.

The agent was waiting for Jack and opened the door before he had time to knock. "I saw you and your wolf when you got out of the car. Besides, Mr. Conners called and let me know that you were on your way. By the way, I'm agent Beverly Senchel," Beverly said as she reached for the bag that Jack was carrying and began pulling everything out of the bag.

"Man, I'm not believing this. I didn't pull anything out of the bag at Mr. Conners' office. He just told me that I would be dressing like an old lady and Chain would be dressing up too. But this is too much," Jack said in disbelief.

"It may help get the job done though," Beverly said while trying not to laugh.

"Do you mean to tell me that we have matching outfits?" Jack asked.

"Yes you do. You both have a pink straw hat and Chain has a purple polka dotted coat and you have a purple polka dotted dress," Beverly replied as she took Jack's outfit out of the bag.

"Well I don't have time to go and buy a new disguise, so I guess this will have to do," Jack said as he reached for his outfit.

While Jack was in the bathroom dressing he wondered why he hadn't ever met Beverly. He had heard that she was small but tough. She didn't look to be over five feet tall and probably didn't weigh one hundred pounds soaking wet. Jack had to admit that she was kind of cute with her short blond hair and blue eyes. She didn't look like a police officer at all. *That's good, though, she won't have any problem working under cover*, he thought as he stepped out of the bathroom wearing his pink straw hat and purple polka-dotted dress and white orthopedic shoes.

"Come sit down in this chair and let me put your make-up and wig on. Both of us will work on Chain," Beverly said, smiling. "Oh, by the way, did you get your wires on alright?" she asked.

"Yeah, I think so,"replied Jack.

"Let me check just to be sure," Beverly said while unzipping Jack's dress and checking the wires. "Yeah, you're ready," she added.

"You might as well go ahead and laugh. I'd laugh myself if I saw someone else wearing this get-up," Jack said as he sat down.

"It's good that you have a sense of humor," Beverly said as she began applying Jack's make-up.

"It's just that I want to put an end to the drugs in my home town. When I see young children dying from drugs, then what I'm wearing doesn't matter that much," Jack said while trying to convince himself that the clothes he was wearing weren't that bad.

Chain didn't resist getting wired and dressed up, which surprised Jack since Chain hadn't ever worn clothes. Maybe he sensed that it was part of his job since his master was wearing a dress the same design as his coat.

"Let's get going, Chain," Jack said as soon as Chain was wired and dressed.

"You both look absolutely smashing," said Beverly as she put a pair of black sunshades on Chain.

"Wait a minute, boy," Jack said laughing so hard that he could hardly talk.

"Do you mean that this whole get-up that you and your wolf are wearing has just struck you as being funny?" Beverly asked now laughing just as hard as Jack.

"I guess so. Now if Chain had pink and purple polka-dotted sunshades instead of black ones then we would really be in business," replied Jack as he made another attempt to leave the motel room.

"I hope things go well for you and your wolf and you're able to catch at least some of the drug pushers in this town," Beverly said as Jack and Chain left the motel room.

"Thanks, so do I," Jack said as he looked at Chain and burst out laughing again.

"I'm sorry, fellow but you are hilarious in that pink straw hat and black sunshades. Your coat is funny but that hat and shades are something else," Jack said as he opened the door of the pink Cadillac so Chain could get in.

Once Jack was in the car he had to sit there for a few minutes to finish calming his laughter. "Let's make sure that we've done everything. We checked our wiring and our back-up team will be waiting. And maybe if I don't look at you I'll be able to drive," Jack said to Chain as he cranked the car. "I don't think Mr. Conners realized what a scene the two of us will be making as we ride through town in these costumes – and in a pink Cadillac at that," Jack told Chain as he drove in the direction of the railroad tracks.

Jack could hear people holler and laugh as they drove past him and Chain. "If we don't accomplish anything else today at least we caused a few people to laugh including myself. When Mr. Conners told me what we would be wearing I should have asked him about the colors," Jack told Chain as he parked the car at the old building near the railroad tracks. Jack practiced talking like a little old lady as he and Chain walked toward the old building. If he wasn't mistaken, that old building used to be an apartment building. The building seemed to be vacant. At least Jack didn't see any cars around. Chain didn't leave Jack's side the entire time they were walking toward the building. Jack felt a little uneasy because everything was so quiet and he could hear Chain growling a very low growl.

The back-up team could hear Chain growling and knew that he and Jack were probably in serious danger. They were prepared to take immediate action at the sign of trouble and continued listening as Jack and Chain got closer to the building. They couldn't help but laugh as they listened to Jack trying to talk like a little old lady. They laughingly kidded among themselves that Chain was probably growling, hoping that Jack would take a hint and be quiet.

Jack had a forty-five in his dress pocket and his hand on it just in case he needed to use it. He was just about to walk in an open door way when he heard someone walk around the right side of the building. Chain didn't move, which surprised Jack.

"Hey granny. Can we help you and your lovely dog?"An older man standing at the left side of the building asked.

"My maid asked me to pick her up here. She said that she lives here. At least I think this is the building. Gee, I'm not sure now if this is the right building or not," Jack said in a squeaky voice.

"You got a cold or something, lady?" asked the younger guy standing propped up against the right side of the building.

"You two are a funny-looking sight," the older man on the left side of the building said before Jack had a chance to answer. "Let's – the three of us and dog makes four – go inside so we can get acquainted and have a little privacy," the older man said.

When they were all in the building, the older man pulled out a gun and asked Jack to give him all his money. Before Jack had a chance to respond Chain jumped the older man and bit the hand that he had the gun in. The gun went off as it fell to the floor and Chain took the bullet in his right leg. The younger man was just about to attack Jack when the back-up team ran in. The young man was so frightened that he told the officers where the drugs were at and names of pushers. The drugs were at another location. The drug pushers only interviewed their prospective buyers at the old building. Jack sure was glad to see his back-up and thanked them as he hugged his wonderful partner.

An ambulance was waiting nearby and responded immediately to their call for help. Chain was showered with loving attention all the way to the veterinarian's office. Dr. Will Simon was informed immediately of his incoming patient so he could have everything ready for emergency surgery if needed on Chain's right leg.

Jack had forgotten all about his date with Penelope until he was sitting in Dr. Simon's waiting room waiting for Chain to get out of surgery and he was thankful that it was only minor surgery. He was also thankful that Beverly had made Chain up so he wouldn't be recognized. If those men had recognized Chain then they might have killed him out of fear.

Jack was deep in thought when Mr. Conners walked into Dr. Simon's office. "Over here," Jack said in his squeaky imitation of a little old lady's voice. Mr. Conners looked at Jack and had to sit down and cover his face with his hands for a few minutes before he could speak. He thought his insides would burst as he tried to hold back his laughter. Jack could see that Mr. Conners was having a hard time trying not to laugh so he whispered in his ear to please go somewhere and call Mattie and tell her not to be alarmed if all of this hits the news before he had time to tell her himself.

Mr. Conners was more than happy to go make a phone call for Jack. That would give him an opportunity to laugh before he burst a gut.

"That man is definitely dedicated to his profession, because there is no way that I would have worn the outfit that he has on," Mr. Conners said to himself as he continued to laugh. A few minutes passed before he calmed down enough to call Mattie. "Tell Jack not to worry about me and that I'll call Penelope and that I will continue to plan the dinner unless he calls and tells me not to," Mattie told Mr. Conners when he finished conveying Jack's message to her.

Mr. Conners went back inside after he finished his phone call with Mattie and whispered to Jack what Mattie asked him to. Jack pulled up his dress sleeve and looked at his watch to check the time and saw it was only three o'clock. He couldn't decide anything until he saw how Chain was going to be. Even though the bullet went right through a fleshy part of Chain's leg, he was still going to need lots of attention until he healed.

Mr. Conners had just finished telling Jack what Mattie said when Dr. Simon came out and told Jack that Chain was going to be fine and that he could take him home. Dr. Simon didn't want Chain to walk on his hurt leg until the next day, so Mr. Conners helped Jack carry Chain out to the car.

"Mr. Conners, I need to get my car. I don't want to keep driving around in that pink Cadillac. I also want to get out of this dress and into my clothes," Jack told Mr. Conners as they were putting Chain into the car.

"Where are your clothes?" Mr. Conners asked while still trying not to laugh.

"They're in the trunk of this pink Cadillac," replied Jack.

"Well, since Dr. Simon and Amanda are the only two people in the office at this time, then get your clothes out of the trunk and go change. I'm sick of looking at you in that outfit myself," Mr. Conners said as he burst into laughter again.

"You picked them out for me to wear," Jack said as he began to laugh too.

"Anyone is allowed one mistake and that was mine. Go get changed now and I'll watch Chain for you," Mr. Conners said as he leaned against the car.

It didn't take Jack long to change and get rid of the wig and make-up. When he finished changing he put the wig, dress, shoes, hat and other clothing into the bag that his clothes were in and walked back out to the car. Mr. Conners was still leaning against the car waiting for Jack.

"Come on Jack, let's go. I'll follow you home and help you get Chain inside the house. Then you can give me the keys to your car and the Cadillac and I'll get a couple of the guys to make the switch for you," Mr. Conners said as he started walking toward his car.

"Sounds good to me. And thanks a lot for what you're doing," Jack said as Mr. Conners got into his car. Mr. Conners just nodded and smiled as he cranked his car.

During the drive home Jack thought about what a wonderful friend and partner Chain had been. Sometimes it seemed as though he knew what Jack needed before Jack himself knew. Jack knew that Chain was torn between him and his desire to be free. Even though Chain had free run in the country since Jack had moved, he still felt obligated to Jack and that was preventing him from being really free. Jack knew that he would someday soon have to set Chain free.

Mattie was so happy to see Jack and Chain home safe. Even though Mattie was still a little uneasy around Chain she had really grown to admire him and it broke her heart to see him hurt.

Mr. Conners drove up right behind Jack and both of them carefully carried Chain inside the house.

"Put Chain right over here next to his food and water bowl. As soon as I heard what happened I went to town and bought him the biggest, softest pillow I could find," Mattie said as she held the kitchen door open for Jack and Mr. Conners.

"Look at this, Chain, my man. Your friend Mattie has fixed you a really soft bed so you can be comfortable while you heal," Jack said as he and Mr. Conners carefully laid Chain on his pillow.

"Mr. Conners, won't you sit down and have a cup of coffee or something before you leave?" Jack asked as he handed him the keys to the Cadillac and his car.

"I really need to get back to the office and get a couple of the guys to get your car and get the Caddy back to where it belongs," replied Mr. Conners.

"Well, thanks for everything," Jack said as he walked outside with Mr. Conners.

"Don't give it another thought. After all you and Chain are responsible for putting a drug supplier and his gang behind bars and I don't mind doing anything that I can for you or Chain," Mr. Conners said as he cranked his car to leave.

Jack looked down at his watch as he turned to walk back into the house and saw that he only had a couple of hours to get ready for his date with Penelope. Mattie already had the table set with white candles in the silver candle holders that Jack's mother had left for Allie. Allie had forgotten all about the candle holders so Mattie didn't see any harm in putting them to some use. Mattie had planned a green salad, spaghetti, Italian bread and red wine for Jack and Penelope's dinner. *Everything will be just perfect for the occasion*, Mattie thought as she hurried around in the kitchen trying to make certain that everything was perfect.

Jack thought about the wedding rings that his mother had left for him in her will. She wanted him to give them to the woman that he would someday fall in love with and marry. He had thought that it would be Wendy, but that didn't work out. Wendy never saw the rings, but hopefully Penelope would agree to marry him and then he would put them on her finger and they would remain there for the rest of their lives. Jack really believed in the "until death do us part" marriage vows.

While Jack showered and dressed for his date with Penelope she was doing the same at her apartment. She was trying to get herself and Charley ready. In the meantime Mattie was putting the final touches on the dinner she had so lovingly prepared.

"Gee, everything smells just great," Jack said as he walked into the kitchen.

"Is it that late already?" Mattie asked as she noticed that Jack was already to leave to go get Penelope.

"I tried to get ready a little early because I want to sit and talk with you a little while before I have to leave," Jack replied as he put his arm around Mattie.

"Oh yeah. What do you want to talk to me about?" Mattie asked as she gave Jack a warm motherly hug.

"I just want to thank you for what you're doing for me. Not only for what you're doing now, but for everything that you have done. You have been like a mother to me and that means a lot. I want you to continue on keeping house for me even if Penelope and I get married. You know that Penelope has grown to love you like a mother too and we just wouldn't be as happy without you in our lives," Jack said as he watched Mattie's wonderful face light up.

"I've enjoyed to the fullest everything that I have done for you and Penelope and you know that I truly love little Charley. I enjoy watching Charley while Penelope works and I feel like the three of you are my children. You have made me feel useful at a time when I need to feel useful the most," Mattie said as she gave Jack a great big hug.

"Well, you just continue on being a part of our lives and believe me, you will feel useful all the time because we really do need you and we don't know what we would do without you," Jack said as he checked his shirt pocket to see if his mother's wedding rings were still in there.

"You had better get going, honey, if you don't want to be late. It's six-thirty and a girl don't like to be kept waiting," Mattie said as she playfully shooed Jack out the door.

"See you later, Chain. Try and eat something while I'm gone," Jack said as he walked out the door.

"He'll be fine. You just enjoy this afternoon and tonight and leave everything else to me," Mattie said as she walked with him to the car.

Mr. Conners had kept his word and gotten someone to swap out cars for Jack. Now Jack felt like a school boy in love for the first time as he got in his car to go get Penelope. His palms were sweaty and he felt a lump in the pit of his stomach. He knew Penelope loved him, but what if after all she had been through in the past had caused her to fear a permanent relationship

Penelope was ready when Jack got to her house and Charley greeted him with open arms and a big kiss. She was growing so fast and Jack really hoped that he would be a good father to her if Penelope agreed to marry him. Jack had the good fortune of having two good parents and he wanted that for his children. He already loved Charley and knew that love wouldn't be the problem. "Come on girls, let's get going," said Jack playfully as he opened the front door for Penelope and Charley.

Jack looked with pride and happiness as he watched Penelope lovingly carry Charley out to the car. He knew that she would continue to be a good mother to Charley and a good mother to any children they might have.

"Mattie told me that she would bring Charley back here to your place so that we could have dinner alone. I hope that's okay," Jack asked Penelope as he opened the car door for her to put Charley's car seat in.

"It would be nice to have an uninterrupted dinner for a change. Don't get me wrong, I love Charley and I love the time that we spend together but everybody needs an occasional break," replied Penelope.

Mattie had her own and Charley's dinner fixed to take to Penelope's by the time Jack drove up. Mattie held the kitchen door open and yelled out for Jack to put Charley's car seat in her car. "You might as well just go ahead and put Charley in the car too, because I'm ready to leave," Mattie continued to yell out the door.

Jack moved the car seat with Charley in it from his car to Mattie's while Mattie got her purse and the to-go dinners. "Do you need some help?" Penelope asked Mattie as she saw her walking toward the car with both hands full. "You can take these two dinners and set them in the front passenger seat for me. Charley and I will dine together when we get to your place. You need to go ahead and give me your house key too," replied Mattie.

Penelope gave Mattie her house key and she and Jack watched her drive away with Charley safely buckled in her car seat before going into the house. Both of them silently hoped that Mattie knew that they really did appreciate her and everything she does for them.

" I don't want to stay too late. Mattie's not a spring chicken anymore and I know she must already be tired from cooking and cleaning," Penelope said as she tenderly took hold of Jack's hand.

"Give her time to get to your house and then call her and invite her to spend the night. Then she can go to bed whenever she wants to," Jack said as he led Penelope toward the house.

"I'll have to borrow your house key because I haven't had time to get anymore made. I need to get Mattie another one made, she can't find the one I gave her," Penelope said as she stepped into the kitchen.

Once Penelope was in the kitchen she walked over to Chain, knelt down on the floor beside him and gently stroked his head and back and told him how proud she was of him for saving Jack's life. "You're such a wonderful friend and partner to Jack and everyone loves you so much," Penelope said as she continued to rub his head and back.

"Watch him take in all that petting. He's all laid back taking in every bit of it,' Jack said with a slight giggle as he refilled Chain's food and water bowl.

"He's entitled to enjoy bad health until he gets well," Penelope laughingly said as she left Chain's bedside to walk into the dining room.

Penelope stood in wide eyed amazement at a wonderful job Mattie did with the dining room table. The white lace table cloth looked beautiful with the silver candle holders that held long white tapered candles. Mattie had left the spaghetti and bread warming, the salad in the fridge, and the wine chilling so all that Jack had to do was fix his and Penelope's plates and pour their wine. Penelope could see the love that went into everything Mattie had done and she was very touched.

"Jack, come see how lovely the table looks. Mattie has arranged everything so beautifully for us," Penelope said appreciatively.

"I know, I saw it earlier. She is truly a loving and caring person and I hope she knows that it is appreciated," Jack said as he held out a chair and gestured for Penelope to sit down.

"I know we pay her, but I would like to do something really nice for her," Penelope said as she inhaled the aroma of the dinner.

"It does smell good, doesn't it?" Jack asked as poured Penelope and himself a glass of wine. While they sipped their wine, Jack fixed his and Penelope's salads and served the rest of their dinner.

"The dinner surely does smell good," Penelope said as she licked her lips as though she couldn't wait to eat.

Jack watched Penelope as she ate and thought about how wonderful it would be to have dinner together like that every night. He was also silently preparing a marriage proposal. *Well I might as well just speak from the heart and hope for the best*, Jack thought to himself.

"Penelope, you know that I love you and Charley and that I would protect the both of you with my life," Jack said as he reached for her hand.

"I know you do and I love you too," Penelope said with a hint of curiosity in her voice.

"Well, here goes. What I want to know is: will you marry me?" Jack asked with a heart full of hope.

"I really want to, but are you sure that you can live with everything that has happened to me in the past?" Penelope asked in reply.

"If I wasn't sure then I wouldn't be asking you to marry me. And Penelope, there is one thing that I want you to remember and never forget; and that is you had no control over what happened to you and what happened to you didn't change the wonderful person that you are," Jack said as he lovingly looked into her eyes.

"Well, if you're sure, then the answer is yes," Penelope said as tears of joy filled her eyes.

"You have made me the happiest man in the world, and I would like for us to get married right out back in my flower garden in two weeks with just a few close friends and what few family members that we have. Feel free to invite your father if you want to," Jack said as tears of happiness filled his eyes too.

"Whatever you want, you sweet, wonderful man; however, I choose not to invite my father," Penelope said as she broke down and cried tears of pure joy.

"If you don't want to invite your father then you don't have to. But right now just close your eyes and hold out your left hand," Jack said as he reached in his shirt pocket and pulled out his mothers engagement ring and wedding band. With Penelope's eyes closed Jack slipped the engagement ring on her hand. Penelope opened her eyes as she felt the ring go on her finger.

"That was my mother's and so was this wedding band that I'll be putting on your hand in two weeks," Jack said as he looked intently into Penelope's beautiful, tear-stained eyes.

"Oh Jack, this ring is absolutely out-of-this-world gorgeous. I'll never take it off," Penelope said as she and Jack both got out of their chairs and wrapped their arms around each other.

"Not trying to get off the subject of us, but we didn't call Mattie and tell her that she could spend the night at your place," Jack said as he remembered that Mattie was babysitting Charley.

"I'll do that right now," Penelope said as she rubbed her engagement ring while scurrying over to the telephone.

Jack poured Penelope and himself another glass of wine while she was calling Mattie. While Penelope was talking to Mattie, Jack was recalling the events of the day as he slowly sipped his wine. The day had been very eventful, to say the least. He hoped his name didn't appear in the paper along with Chain's. It seemed rather pointless for him to do undercover work if the media was just going to find out his name and put it in the paper. Even though this was going to be his last undercover job he still didn't like for his name to be in the paper. Jack told Mr. Conners that if Penelope agreed to marry him, then he wanted a desk job. Mr. Conners told Jack how valuable that he and Chain were to the force, but if that was really what he wanted then he would try and make an opening for him in the office.

"Jack, I have to go home. Mattie thinks that Charley has a fever," Penelope said as she hung up the phone.

"Did Mattie check Charley's temperature to be sure?" Jack asked with an unmistakable note of concern in his voice.

"She said that she couldn't see the numbers on the thermometer, however Charley's skin felt rather warm," Penelope replied anxiously.

"Well, let's not waste time talking, let's go see about Charley," Jack said as he slipped his arm around Penelope and led her toward the door.

"See you later Chain. You'll be fine 'til I get home," Jack said as he closed the door behind himself.

Jack could see Mattie looking out the window as he drove up in front of Penelope's house. *Poor Mattie's beside herself with worry*, Jack thought to himself as he and Penelope got out of the car. Jack could feel Penelope trembling as he put his arm around her to escort her to the house.

"I was afraid to give the poor little darling any medicine," Mattie said as soon as Jack and Penelope stepped inside the house.

"Don't worry, Mattie, children have fevers occasionally. I'll check on her right now, but I'm sure she'll be fine," Penelope said trying to calm Mattie's fears as she headed toward Charley's room.

"I was just getting ready to dial your number when Penelope called me," Mattie told Jack.

"I'm sorry that Charley feels bad, but it's not your fault,"Jack said, also trying to reassure Mattie.

"Charley only has a little fever. I gave her something for her fever, and if she isn't any better in the morning then I'll take her to her doctor," Penelope said as she rejoined Jack and Mattie in the living room.

"I'm glad Charley's going to be fine, but if I'm not needed here, then I need to go on back home and see about Chain," Jack said as he walked over to hug Penelope.

"We'll be fine here. You need to go on back home and see about Chain. That poor baby has had a rough day and he deserves a lot of attention," Penelope said as she returned Jack's hug.

"Don't you worry about Penelope and Charley. I'll stay the night with them and we will be just fine," Mattie said as she excused herself from the room so Jack and Penelope could have a little privacy while they said their goodnights.

Penelope and Mattie sat up for a little while after Jack left and made wedding plans. Penelope had never dreamed than any man would ever love her as much as Jack did. Mattie assured Penelope that she was getting a wonderful husband and friend. Penelope sat and rubbed her engagement ring as she told Mattie how happy she was.

"It has been a long day and I need to get some sleep," Mattie said as she got up off the sofa and walked over to Penelope to give her a goodnight hug.

"I'm sorry, I didn't mean to keep you up with my plans," Penelope said as she returned Mattie's hug.

"Don't apologize, honey. I've enjoyed listening to your plans and I'm so glad to see the two of you so happily in love," Mattie said as she excused herself to retire for the night.

As soon as Jack got home he checked on Chain and made sure the house was locked for the night and went to bed himself. Jack fell asleep while recalling his life as a police officer and then as an undercover drug investigator. *Some undercover*, he thought. Most everyone knew who he was, and now Chain was a celebrity – and rightly so. He had already saved two children's lives and now his. "What I want to do is to set him free and I do mean really free before he gets killed," Jack said thinking out loud.

Chain awoke Jack the next morning, licking his hand. "How are you doing my main man?" Jack asked Chain as he checked on his leg. Chain just growled his happy growl as Jack got out of bed and made his way into the kitchen.

"You're hungry, aren't you, boy?" Jack asked as he filled his food and water bowl. While Chain was eating Jack walked outside on the front porch to get the morning paper. Mattie drove up just as Jack was walking back into the house.

"Good, Mattie's here. Now I can find out how Charley's doing without calling and waking Penelope," Jack said to himself as he walked into the kitchen. "How's Charley this morning?" Jack asked Mattie as she opened the kitchen door to walk inside.

"She's fine. Penelope got up and checked her temperature before I left and she didn't have any fever, so she went back to bed since she didn't have to work today," Mattie said as she sat her purse on the kitchen table and made her way to the kitchen sink to run water for the coffee pot.

"I'm sure glad to hear that the little darling is alright," Jack said as he held up the front page of the newspaper so Mattie could see the headlines.

"Read the article to me while I fix breakfast," Mattie said as she plugged in the coffee pot and then reached to open the fridge to take out the bacon and eggs.

"Alright, here goes. Headlines are, 'Chain, Jack McCain's Wolf Has Saved Another Life. This time, his owners'. Without the help of this magnificent animal, Jack would not be alive and we would not have been able to confiscate thousands of dollars worth of drugs and capture the leader of the drug ring, along with his assistants. Rumor has it that Jack and Chain were dressed for the occasion, but we won't write about that. The community is very proud of Jack and Chain for their fight against drugs. We also want to take this opportunity to publicly thank the both of them.' That's it," Jack said as he finished reading the article.

"That's a very nice article," Mattie said as she poured Jack and herself a cup of coffee.

"I guess so, but I'm just tired of making the headlines," Jack said as he laid the newspaper on the table.

"I can understand that. But you and Chain both deserve some recognition for risking your lives the way you do," Mattie said while preparing breakfast.

"I don't do it for recognition. I really want a drug-free place to live and raise a family," Jack said as he reached for his coffee cup.

"I know you do, honey," Mattie said softly.

Chapter Eight

Two weeks had passed, and it was May seventh, Jack and Penelope's wedding day. The flower garden in Jack's back yard was beautiful. Numerous flowers of all kinds are in full bloom. The walkway that lead to the gazebo had a seven-foot arch, covered with running vines and different kinds of flowers. The lattice work on the beautiful white gazebo was also covered with different kinds of flowers. The back lawn was freshly mowed and the air was filled with the aroma of freshly cut grass, honeysuckles and other flowers. The sun was shining brightly, the sky was blue with only a few small white clouds that looked as though they were painted on the sky. The light cool breeze that was blowing only made for a more beautiful morning. Jack and Penelope planned to say their marriage vows in the gazebo with a Justice of the Peace performing the wedding ceremony.

Allie and her son Jimmy arrived a couple of days early so they could spend some time with Jack. Allie's husband, Jeff couldn't make it because of an emergency at the airline where he worked. Apparently a few of the crew contracted a virus and Jeff had to take one of the pilot's place on a flight to Greece.

Penelope arrived at Jack's house with Charley a couple of hours before the wedding and used the guest room to get dressed. She already had her hair and make-up done, so all she had to do was to get Charley and herself dressed.

Jack hired a caterer for the wedding reception and everything was on schedule as planned. There were only thirty people invited to the wedding, and only twenty were planning to come. That was all right with Jack, because he was nervous enough anyway. Jack and Penelope wrote their own vows and they only hoped that they would remember them and not have to read them in front of everyone.

Mattie had agreed to be Penelope's matron of honor, Jimmy the ring bearer, Charley the flower girl and of course, Mr. Conners the best man.

The moment had finally arrived and both Jack and Penelope were as nervous as they could possibly be. The guest had arrived and were seated and were waiting for the wedding to take place.

Jack and Mr. Conners were standing in their proper place and when "Here Comes The Bride" began to play all heads turned and all eyes became intently fixed on the back door as everyone eagerly awaited to see the bride. Everyone was amazed at Penelope's beauty as she so gracefully walked down the garden path in the lovely white gown that she had so carefully chosen for what she hoped with all her heart would be a perfect day. Penelope chose to wear her hair down, since Jack liked it better down. Her black hair really shone against her white wedding gown, and her gold heart necklace and gold bracelet complimented her engagement ring. She wasn't overdressed, and her natural beauty was obvious to everyone as she slowly walked toward her one true love with the genuine hope of spending the rest of her life with him. Her heart seemed to melt when she saw him standing next to Mr. Conners. Knowing what a kind and loving person he was made her love him even more. She knew without a doubt that he was the most handsome man in the world, and she felt very fortunate to have him in her life.

Jack felt his heart do flip-flops as he watched Penelope walking toward him. He sincerely hoped that his love would make her forget all the bad things that had happened to her. He desperately wanted to be the best husband and father that he could possibly be.

The wedding ceremony was beautiful and even more so as Jack and Penelope said their vows.

"I, Jack McCain, take you, Penelope Augustine, to be my lawfully wedded wife, in sickness and in health, for better or for worse, and hopefully forever. Since I met you, my days have been filled with hope for a better and happier future. I'm not lonely anymore, because even when I'm alone my thoughts are filled with love and hope for a happy future with you. I only hope that I make you the kind of husband that you will be proud of. I promise never to be too busy to talk to or listen to you. I promise to love you always with all my heart, soul and mind forever," Jack vowed as he slipped the wedding band on Penelope's left ring finger.

"I, Penelope Augustine, take you, Jack McCain, to be my lawfully wedded husband, in sickness and in health, for better or for worse, forever. Trusting you with my life was the best thing I ever did. Now I'm trusting you with my life again, and I know that you will never disappoint me. When I look into your eyes, I see love, hope and joy, and you have made me the happiest woman in the world by wanting to share your life with me. I'll love you with all my heart, soul and mind, forever," Penelope vowed as she slipped the wedding band on Jack's left ring finger.

Everyone at the wedding had misty eyes as the Justice of the Peace pronounced Jack and Penelope husband and wife.

No one noticed the unexpected guests at the wedding until Jack kissed the bride. Chain, the white wolf and seven little pups were at the edge of the yard, and they seemed to be watching the wedding. However, when the white wolf noticed the guests looking her way she disappeared back into the woods with her pups following along behind her. Chain looked at Jack and hesitated, before following his family. Jack didn't try to stop Chain because he knew that he would be back.

When the reception was over, Mattie took Charley home with her so the happy couple could go on their one-week honeymoon to Hawaii. Allie agreed to stay and watch Chain and the house for the week that they were gone.

During the plane ride, Jack discussed with Penelope his feelings about setting Chain free and his decision to retire as an undercover drug investigator.

"Chain has been a great partner and friend, however I know in my heart that he longs to be free. I know he's an animal, but sometimes I swear he knows what I think and feel and I have this gut feeling that I'm going to have to tell Chain that he's free to go. I also want a normal married life and I know that an office job can give me that," Jack said as he looked into Penelope's eyes.

"Jack, I trust you to make the right decision where your profession and Chain are concerned," Penelope said as she squeezed his hand with all the love she felt in her heart.

The week went by so quickly that they didn't have a chance to see all the sights that they wanted to. Before they knew it, they were back home and unpacking. Charley was thrilled to see her mother and Jack and greeted them with a big hug and kiss. Seeing how happy Charley was to see him made Jack realize the need to adopt Charley.

The next morning after Allie and Jimmy left for home Jack and Penelope discussed Jack adopting Charley. She needed a daddy and Jack wanted to make it official by adopting her.

Jack and Penelope's discussion was interrupted by a local news bulletin.

"The lives of a family of four has been saved by what appeared to be a wolf. At three o'clock this morning the man of the house heard the sound of breaking glass and an animal howling. The power was out, due to an electrical storm the night before and their smoke detector didn't go off. The man admits to being frightened when he awoke to see what appeared to be a wolf in the doorway of his bedroom. The animal was howling and moving around as if he were trying to tell him something. At that time he smelled smoke and the fear of the animal was gone and a deeper fear took over. He knew that he had to get his wife and kids out of the house and did so immediately. When a local reporter asked the man and his wife if they believed that the animal was Jack McCain's wolf, they said that it looked like him. They had a large battery-operated light on in the hallway and could see the animal fairly well. Once the animal saw that the man was out of bed, he went out the same way that he came in, through a window that he had broken to get in. There was a large fire in the kitchen that was apparently caused by the storm," said the local news announcer as they returned to their regular scheduled program.

"Do you suppose that Chain saved that family?" Penelope asked.

"It's possible. I couldn't get him to come inside last night so I just let him run free. If that was him that saved that family then it's a good thing that I did let him run free," replied Jack, knowing that it was time to really set Chain free. "Penelope, I'm going outside to get the morning paper and check on Chain. I hope that he's outside," Jack said as he walked toward the front door. "Man, everything smells wonderful after a good rain," Jack said, thinking out loud as he bent down to pick up the newspaper.

With paper in hand, Jack walked around to the back of the house calling for Chain. Chain came out of the woods with a little gray wolf pup following him, while the white wolf remained at the edge of the yard with the remaining six pups.

"Come here, my main man," Jack said as Chain came running to him. When Jack bent over to give Chain a welcome home hug he could feel and see small pieces of glass in his hair. He knew then that Chain had been the one to save that family. Chain licked Jack's hand and playfully jumped around for a few seconds and then looked toward the white wolf and their pups and made a dash toward them. The little gray wolf pup tried to catch up with Chain, but Chain stopped running and turned around and began nudging the pup back in Jack's direction. Jack suddenly realized what Chain was trying to do. Chain was trying to tell Jack good-bye and he wanted to give him one of his pups to take his place. Jack ran over to Chain and hugged him while he tried to get the glass out of his hair.

"You crazy, wonderful friend, I really hate to let you go. But if you insist, then I have to respect your wishes. You're just as entitled to be happy as I am. I can see that you want to be with your family as much as I want to be with mine. Go on, my friend, and be happy," Jack said as tears began to fill his eyes and as he hugged Chain for the last time. Jack felt like his heart would burst as he felt an overwhelming sense of loss as he released Chain from his embrace and watched him turn and run toward the woods.

As Jack bent down and scooped up Chain's little pup in his hands he realized that the pup was a male. Chain wanted to give him one of his sons to raise as he had raised him. Jack sadly watched Chain turn around to look one last time at his master and one of his pups and what had once been his home then he disappeared into the woods to join his family. When Chain was completely out of sight, Jack took Chain II into the house to meet his new family.

Penelope, Charley and Mattie welcomed Chain II to the family with a big hug. It seemed to Jack that Mattie had finally overcome her fear of animals. If she hadn't, then she was doing a good job of hiding them from him, because she sure seemed happy that Chain II was going to be part of the family.

Cliff Crowley died in jail from a massive heart attack. Jack adopted Charley. Mattie continued on as Jack and Penelope's housekeeper, babysitter and friend. Jack got his office job but continued to do a little undercover work from time to time. Will Simon is now Chain II's vet with his wife, Amanda, as his assistant. Allie, Jeff and Jimmy continued to visit from time to time.

Sometimes at night, Jack hears Chain and his family howling in the distance, and occasionally Chain makes the headlines in the local newspaper and a few times in the world news when he rescues someone from a harmful situation. He is now known everywhere as "Chain, King of the Wolves" and rightly so, because he continues to risk his own life to save others.

Printed in the United States
27671LVS00006B/1-18

9 781413 740486